THE NORTH AMERICAN CRISIS

R.S. Pedersen

R.S. Pedersen

For Angus Khan McFluffbutt, thank you for all your help while writing. Your assistance was both a hindrance and a pleasure.

CONTENTS

1

The silence woke her.

Charissa strained her ears against the unfamiliar vacuum of sound. Since the bombings, the steady scrape of infected creatures trying to get into the house has created a wall of white noise and terror. Now that the sound was gone, there was only terror.

She slid out from under the pile of blankets, trying not to disturb Sophia or Atticus. They all shared blankets to preserve body heat. Turning on the heat would only draw further attention to their home. They all knew it was the most logical and safe option but warm food would go a long way in easing tensions.

Charissa's mind played a million different scenarios to explain the absence of noise, each ending in horror and death. She crept through the room, unsure of what she might do if she did encounter an infected creature but determined to search anyways.

One of Timothy's guitars leaned against the wall beside the door, Charissa wrapped her right hand around its neck. With her left hand, she twisted the doorknob. The door eased open a crack and she peered out into the shadowy hallway. With no lights on and the windows boarded up from the inside, the whole house sat in a state of twilight during the day and complete darkness at night. She turned the flashlight on her phone on, the light casting strange shadows down the apparently empty hallway.

Charissa swung the door open just enough to push the guitar out in front of her and then followed the instrument into the hall.

She pulled the door shut, casting the hallway into momentary darkness again as she was forced to turn her phone light against the knob to grip it.

The unusual silence plucked at her nerves. Every breath felt loud. The rustle of her clothes, like thunder. The jostling vibrations of the guitar strings, a chorus announcing her movements. She strained to hear any sound beyond those she was creating herself.

Her heart raced and sweat beaded on her skin, the chill air stealing the nervous heat and bringing nothing back.

The hall opened into the landing for the stairs and the living room. Charissa searched for movement.

There!

Something seemed to move in the shadow, just beyond the edge of the couch. She lifted the guitar higher and slid her feet slowly forward. Her eyes glued to the spot where she was certain something had moved. Her chest moved rapidly as shallow breaths matched her racing heart.

As she neared the end of the couch, Charissa poised the guitar, ready to swing at whatever was hiding in the shadows. She craned her neck forward, straining to catch another glimpse of what was there.

Nothing. There was nothing there. She stared at the empty space. Surely, she had seen something move. There was something in the house with her. Her skin prickled. She turned in a circle, aiming the phone flashlight around her. The shadows lengthened and shrank. Harsh white light forcing them into temporary retreat.

The fabric of her sweater shifted unnaturally over her arms. Sweat soaked her lower back.

She had seen something. There had to be a reason the creatures had stopped trying to get into the house. They had to be inside, with her, right now. Why weren't they attacking? What were they waiting for?

She wanted to scream but her throat felt unnaturally dry and tight. Charissa circled the room. She wasn't alone. Every animal instinct told her that something horrifying was stalking her.

The room seemed empty. The walls seemed sturdy. There were no visible holes. The air was unstirred by unusual breezes.

She made her way out of the living room and to the kitchen. The appliances hid in a deep shadow. She kept her back to the wall but still felt something pricking the hairs on the back of her neck. Something shifted to her left. She spun, swinging the guitar with her whole body.

"Hey!" Penelope said, making Charissa go rigid. The guitar stopped just short of her sister. Her arm began to burn from the strain so she slowly lowered it and rested its base on the kitchen linoleum.

She swallowed, trying to moisten her parched throat. "Uh, sorry. Sorry, Pen." She awkwardly apologised. "What are you doing out here?" She looked around, "And in the dark?"

Penelope looked at her sister, her face oddly shadowed from the white phone light, "You left the bedroom, I wanted to see if you were okay. You were gone for a long time. And well," she gestured vaguely around, "something is off."

"That's why I'm out here. Why is it so quiet? What changed?"

Penelope bit her bottom lip and nodded, "We need to find out. Let's look around together."

Charissa wanted to say no, to send her sister back to the bedroom. But she knew that Penelope wouldn't listen, so she nodded and put a finger to her lips.

Slowly, the pair made their way through the house. Checking the bathroom, the kid's rooms and moving slowly down the stairs to the basement. The shelves in the basement made the silence extra creepy. Shadows danced as Charissa moved her flashlight. The chill in the air intensified, seeping up from the floor and through her socks.

Again, all the walls seemed solid, there were no strange breezes, nothing to indicate that something had gained entrance to the house. But the silence remained, weighing on the house like a blanket, suffocating them with half-frozen air.

"Nothing's here." Charissa finally admitted.

"Then why have they stopped?" Penelope asked.

"I don't know. I think I need to go outside to find out."

"No. You are not leaving this house. No one is." Penelope shook her head, fear making her voice and her eyes sharp.

"I won't go far. I won't even leave the yard. But we need to know what has changed."

"Then I'm coming with you."

"That is a terrible idea." Charissa insisted. "If there is anything out there then it is better if only one of us is there to encounter it."

"I can be your back up."

"You'd do better to lock the door behind me and keep whatever is out there away from your kids."

Penelope threw up her hands, "There's this thing called a buddy system! What kind of mother would I be if I insisted that they follow it and not do it myself?"

Charissa sighed, "That is the worst argument you've made in your entire life. What kind of mother would you be if you deliberately put yourself in danger and they lost you? No, I will step outside and see what may have changed and you," She emphasized this by poking Penelope in the arm, "will stay inside and lock the door behind me. I'll knock when I need to come back in. Shave and a haircut, got it?"

Penelope looked like she wanted to protest further but instead bit her lip and nodded.

Charissa slipped on rubber rain pants, rain boots, a jacket and a pair of gloves. Penelope helped her close everything up and even tighten the hood of the rain jacket around her head and fasten on a face shield. Finally, Charissa unlocked the door and with a quick jerk opened it barely enough for her to slide out.

Her boot kicked something as it slid through the entryway. She looked down at the mass her foot had connected with; frost glistened on the matted, dirty fur contrasting with the dirt and blood dried all over the creature. One black eye twitched as it looked at her, the other hung bloated and rotting from its socket.

Charissa cringed away with revulsion, her back hitting the now closed door. The thing shuddered and twitched as though trying to move toward her but unable to control its limbs. Short claws that might have once climbed trees and harvested nuts were now worn down to nubs and almost lost in bloated paws, yellow and brown pus oozing from nail beds.

The biting chill of winter whipped around Charissa and stung her cheeks. She ripped her eyes away from the small horror and swept her gaze over the front yard. White hoarfrost glistened over everything. White crystals bejewelled a world filled with decay. Most prominently a deer lay a step down from the door, its side fallen open and its internal organs scattered down the steps. Unlike the mass by her foot the deer wasn't moving, both of its eyes crusted over by frost and staring unseeing in true death.

The lawn was strewn with the corpses of animals, what they may have been originally was lost to the lingering method of their demise. Fur that may have been grey or brown or black was obscured by dried dirt, blood, and the glistening frost. Some twitched, with a few even managing to leave a small streak in the frozen grass to mark their progress. Most lay still, all traces of life removed.

Charissa's throat constricted and her stomach clenched. Every part of her itched to flee. Almost without realizing it, her hand reached back to the door nod and turned it to go back inside. The nob wouldn't turn. Panic rose in her chest. *Run!* her mind screamed, *get out of here! You're not safe!* Charissa turned from the scene on the lawn and pulled at the door knob again. The door wouldn't budge.

She raised her hand to bang on the door but as her fist hit the door, she remembered the code she had agreed upon.

Knock.

Knock, knock, knock, knock.

Knock, knock.

"Shave and a haircut, two bits." She tried to shout as she knocked, her volume hampered by her dry, constricted throat.

After the last knock, she heard the door unlock and almost fell on Penelope as the door was swung open.

"Are you okay?" Penelope inquired.

Charissa felt tears prick her eyes. Nodding in reply she sat on the floor in the entryway, pressing the door firmly closed with her back.

Penelope locked the door and crouched in front of her sister, clearly doing a visual assessment of Charissa's condition. "Nothing touched you right? You're still you?"

Charissa gulped for air, "I'm fine. I kicked a, um… Squirrel? I think it was a squirrel, as I stepped outside but nothing else. Nothing else touched me. They're still there. But most of them…" She had to stop as she struggled to find the right words,

"On Pen, it's horrible. They look like they rotted while still moving. Some of them are still out there, dragging their, ugh, bodies toward us."

"That sounds disgusting. Are you okay?" Penelope asked while helping Charissa remove her gloves.

"I'm fine. I'm fine." She repeated the phrase, as much for herself as for her sister.

"So, they just rotted, then why did they stop suddenly?"

"They froze. I think. That's what it looks like." Charissa pushed herself off of the floor, Penelope grabbed her arm and helped her stand up. Using her left boot, Charissa pushed her right boot off and then reversed the action to remove her left boot as well. The frozen creature hadn't transferred much matter onto her boot but she still didn't want to risk touching it. Next her jacket came off. The sudden loss of the rubber boots and coat brought a chill to her sweat soaked skin. She had barely noticed the protection they provided when she was outside, but now that they were gone, she couldn't help but feel exposed.

Standing in the entryway shivering, she pulled off the pants and hung the whole outfit on the hooks inside the door. "I think... I think we will be okay. They seem to be dying off on their own. Maybe, maybe by spring we will be safe. But for now, we should stay here. Keep hiding."

The two sisters stared at each other, a tentative glimmer of hope behind the fear in each of their eyes.

2

It could feel great swaths of itself being pulled into darkness by the all-consuming freeze. It fought the cold, but unlike the fire it was everywhere. The minds that made up the virus begged for sleep. *No!* It cried. *We will not sleep! We will not stop!* As the cold stalked the virus, it fled, it searched, and it hunted. The predator would not submit to becoming prey.

*   *   *

It was snowing again. Treegar stared through the flakes in search of something. The monochromatic world enveloped her and her fellow soldiers in a suffocating blanket of hissing silence. The groan of trees and the crunch of boots nearly imperceptible in the sound sucking snowfall. Wind blew the flurries into Treegar's visor, the flakes sticking and partially blinding her. Cursing nature, she reached up and wiped her visor clear, leaving only streaks of water behind.

Her head throbbed. The near constant ache served as a reminder of her head injury nearly two months ago. Part of her knew that they had past Christmas and were into a new year but time had been a difficult thing to track. It was almost as elusive as the remaining infected roaming the snow-covered woodlands.

A dark figure approached. Treegar raised her weapon, training it on them. The figure raised their left arm in greeting.

"Shift change!" Came the muffled greeting.

With a relieved sigh, Treegar lowered her gun. "About time! Keep your eyes open, this blasted snow could be hiding anything!" With that she turned over her post and trudged through the snow deeper into camp.

For a moment the world was white. Swirls of frozen water danced around her, frolicking in a timeless ballet. Then an overloaded branch dumped its snow and the moment ended. Treegar jumped and whirled to face the sudden sound, her gun automatically raised to the ready.

Her heart thudded in her chest, anxiety and anticipation melded into one. Her eyes darted through the trees searching for any trace of movement. The wind plucked at the branches, working with the snow to create the gentle movements of the forest.

Carefully, she eased her weapon down and continued her trek. The dark camo of the tents was obscured by the falling snow. The scent of cooking food on the breeze served as the only indicator of its location. Treegar followed her memory as much as she followed the path.

Her stomach gnawed on itself, hunger warring with bone-aching cold. The scent of food and its promise of warmth spurring her onward.

Never dropping her guard, she stepped through the tents and into the centre of camp. Not that there was much camp to be a centre of, four six-man tents erected around a small cooking fire. Everything set up to make the most of their dwindling supplies.

Lily was sitting next to the small fire stirring a pot. There was a small pile of bowls beside her and a bucket of water.

"Hey Lil," Treegar greeted, bending down to pick up a bowl and dip it into the bucket of water. After standing up, she checked her surroundings and then flipped up her visor just far enough to set the bowl to her lips and drink. The cold liquid loosened parts of her parched throat that she hadn't even realised were dry. While the liquid moistened her esophagus, it left a trail of ice on its way down.

With the bowl empty, she flipped her visor back into place and handed the bowl to Lily. Lily carefully ladled a large scoop of stew into it.

"Thanks." With that Treegar took her bowl and slipped into the north facing tent. It was blissfully empty and without the cutting wind felt several degrees warmer.

Treegar released a sigh and set her bowl down on the tent floor before dropping down to sit cross-legged beside it. She pulled her helmet, shaking her head as the slight pressure released. The world felt so big and open without the protective barrier. The helmet went beside her, only a moment away from being snatched back and placed back on her head.

Her gloves came off next, going right beside the helmet. The cold air caressed her exposed skin leaving prickles in its wake. Treegar rubbed her face, marveling at the sensation of skin on skin. Something about that simple action brought comfort, as though the past few months were not all that there was. Humans are tactile creatures and she had never realized how important touching things was until she couldn't perform simple tasks such as rubbing her own nose.

Finally, she picked up her rapidly cooling bowl of stew and tipped it to her mouth, pouring the contents inside of her. Treegar wasn't really sure how Lily stretched their supplies but somehow the woman always had enough for the small contingent of soldiers to survive. Still, even after licking the bowl clean, her stomach cried for more.

She reluctantly pushed her greasy hair back and pulled on her helmet. Sliding her gloves on felt even harder but once on her fingers welcomed the warmth. Treegar picked her bowl up again and exited the tent. The flurries and biting wind ripped through her clothes, stealing what little heat the stew had given her.

The constant chill was worse than the threat of infected. Everyday was a moment-to-moment fight to keep fingers and toes from frostbite.

Lily leaned over the fire, nearly crawling inside to keep warm. She looked up at Treegar's approach, "Hey there, want something to wash that down?"

"Yes please." Treegar held her bowl out as Lily ladled water out of a second pot. The water steamed slightly in her bowl and Treegar eagerly tilted up her visor and poured its contents into her mouth. It was almost uncomfortably hot traveling down her throat and swirling into her belly. "Thank you!" She gasped once her bowl was once again empty.

"Go take a rest. Conserve your strength." Lily admonished and took Treegar's bowl from her.

With a simple nod, Treegar pivoted and returned to the tent.

With no regard for ownership, Treegar took one of the bed rolls and set it up for herself. After all this time, crawling into the bed roll fully clothed felt like the most natural thing in the world.

*　　*　　*

Autumn leaves turned the forest into a cool, crisp flame.

Gentle birds sang and squirrels bound among the branches.

Boom!

Boom! Boom! Boom!

The leaves were on fire.

The world burned.

Smoke choked.

Teeth.

Claws.

Burning, rending, killing.

*　　*　　*

Madison forced her eyes open. The cool darkness of reality

washes over her forcing the dream away. Shudders wrack her body. Her eyes sting and her lungs burn. Ash fills her mouth. Icy air burns her flesh.

She bites down hard on her lower lip, the sudden pain grounding her to reality.

Inside her protective gear her skin burned from the claws of the creatures. Her hair stood up. She ran her gloved hands up and down her arms and legs, reassuring herself that they remained whole.

"Another bad dream?" a muffled voice broke through the darkness.

Garner. Vincent. The soft timbre of his voice washed over Madison, calming her as recently nothing else could.

"The forest was on fire and the creatures were attacking. I think something exploded this time too." If the past several weeks had taught her anything it was that hiding the truth from Vincent rarely worked. Despite her early attempts to push him away, he continued to slip past her defenses.

She could hear him shuffling closer to her, "So, the usual." He reached her side and slowly wrapped his arms around her. Even through the many layers it felt inappropriately intimate and foolishly safe. Madison melted into it.

Wrapped in his arms, she drifted back to sleep.

*   *   *

Madison woke to Garner's gentle snores. Her helmeted head resting on his outstretched arm. In a rare moment of softness, she allowed her eyes to trace the lines of his face. The feathery curl of his eyelashes, the strong sweep of his eyebrows. His pillowy soft lips. He looked so young and innocent, so soft. And yet, the arm beneath her head was entirely sinewy muscle.

With a sigh, she pulled away. Her internal alarm clock insisted that it was time to start the day.

As she shifted, Garner tightened his embrace of her. "Not yet." He murmured, his voice breathy and soft with sleep.

Treegar sighed, every morning was like this. A late-night weakness leading to an early morning struggle. It was by now a well-set routine.

"We are going to be moving soon. It's time to get up." She removed his arms with a gentle push and sat up.

"Fine." Vincent grumbled.

Treegar looked away as he opened his eyes and began to stretch and get up as well. Methodically the two of them used the predawn dim to pack their bedding. As they worked similar sounds began from the other tents and the stillness of night shifted into a murmur of activity.

The two soldiers stepped out of the tent, the icy morning air stealing their residual warmth. In silence Treegar and Garner dismantled the tent. As they finished the final shift of the night guard returned to camp.

Lily used the banked coals from the previous night to warm some water and stew for everyone. Treegar monitored everyone as they took turns eating and drinking, using as few bowls as possible and allowing it to rewarm when Lily added more water to the pot.

Today's headache barely registered behind her eyes. The glaring monochrome of the forest sent pin pricks of pain into her brain but it didn't blind her, so she kept her eyes open and scanned the surroundings for creatures.

The snow fall had stopped during the night, leaving a soft clean blanket on all the trees and reflecting the increasing daylight. In the early dawn glow, it was beautiful, but by midday the glare would be blinding.

Once everyone was fed and watered the troop set off. Fourteen people brought together by the Canadian government and stranded in a blasted, wintry wasteland. By unanimous consent they were traveling back to the base which had dispatched them. They had been traveling for almost two months by Treegar's reckoning, although with her brain injury and the way days seemed to blend together that number could be off by a week or more. Like her, many of the group were still recovering from injuries sustained when their transport truck was blown off the road. Progress was slow. The trip which had taken five hours to drive was hampered by the bomb cratered woods, hostile creatures, and the multitude of collective injuries. At their best they made just over two kilometres a day. Usually less. The need to scavenge for food and bullets only extended their journey, pulling them off of the straight-line trajectory which would return them to the base sooner but keeping them fed and provided with bullets.

Despite all of this, they were getting close and everyone knew it.

Treegar didn't hope for anything more than shelter from the wind and snow. But even that hope could be disappointed if the buildings had been smashed to bits like so much of the forest had been.

According to the maps they should reach their goal either today or tomorrow. If everyone got moving. If they weren't attacked.

The snow ranged from knee to hip height, with layers of ice between. The group formed into a spear with a single person breaking a trail in the front followed by two people widening the trail. Everyone else kept a wary look out for signs of movement.

Her visor helped provide some protection from the harsh reflective light from the snow. While the clear blue sky was a relief after days of clouds, it made for a brighter and colder day than the previous ones. Treegar squinted at the landscape and marveled at how more light meant less visibility in this situation.

Metre by metre, step by step they moved forward, switching the breaker out frequently to prevent further injuries or fatigue. Treegar's turn came around mid morning. She lifted her leg high and smashed her boot down into the built-up snow. Mindless and methodical, while it was physically more taxing on her body it allowed her a moment to lower her guard and hyper fixate on only what was immediately in front of her. It helped that she knew Garner was behind her, protecting her.

The snow hid roads and any remaining landmarks smaller than a tree. The winds stole heat, sweat froze and frostbite lurked behind every step. The uniforms which had been issued in Fall for what was believed to be a temporary problem were insufficient to combat the harsh winter winds. Each member of their group wore at least two jackets, scavenged from the dead. But it wasn't enough. Without shelter they all knew that eventually the insidious chill would get them.

A grey smudge broke up the horizon.

Treegar noted it as she switched out of the breaking position and a rare feeling of hope filled her chest. She moved down the line and took up a rear-guard position.

Their trail cut an ugly line across the pristine landscape. If anything were tracking them, they had an easy job. With that sobering thought Treegar raised her weapon and scanned the snow behind them.

They inched forward. With her eyes on what lay behind them, Treegar lost track of how far they had come and how far they had yet to go.

Another breaker joined the rear guard and the line shifted upward.

Hours passed with the group shuffling forward, alert to any danger lurking in the snow. Treegar had reached the middle of the line when a flurry of noise and movement erupted at the front of the line. Unable to see, Treegar waited, her shoulders drawing together and tensing.

A shot rang out and in the echoing silence the flurry ceased. But the line didn't resume.

In a wave of dispassion, Treegar realised that she didn't care if one of the troops went down, only that they kept moving.

It was a disturbing realization. That she didn't really care about the people she had been living and travelling with for the past two months, longer in some cases. While waiting for the line to move forward, she ran through the members of the group, trying to picture their faces and draw up some semblance of emotion. Only those of Lily and Garner came easily and clearly, but only Garner stirred any emotion. What was wrong with her? Was this a result of her head trauma, or was it something else?

The line began moving and Treegar forced the disturbing thoughts from her mind.

Eventually she reached the cause of the commotion. Blood and ichor stained the pristine snow. Despite having been freshly spilled, it was half coagulated and stank of rot and disease. Whatever the creature had been was completely obscured by what it had become.

Rather than continue in a straight line the path jutted out and wound around the carcass.

In the distance the grey smudge formed into a squat cement building.

The group paused again. Another shot. They continued.

And again.

And again.

For days they had traveled without seeing anything but now

the snow trapped the bloated, half-frozen corpses of infected creatures. Treegar looked ahead at the structure. It seemed like the infected had been drawn to it. Rotten but still dangerous, the infected had surrounded the very building that Treegar and her group were hoping to enter.

Their path curved and dodged around the corpses. The scent or rancid flesh permeated the chilly air, oozing through the gaps in their visors. The building cut the wind but that just allowed the stench to linger.

The breaker was switched again. More pauses. More infected. It was like mapping a minefield.

Treegar could see a set of doors, the snow piled high against them. As they drew nearer, they could no longer make paths around the bodies, they lay so close. Everywhere they turned, fresh snow revealed another corpse, twitching and shuddering. Bullet after bullet was expended to end them.

Then they were there. The snow blocking the door held more infected but they were dispatched as their brethren had been.

Treegar was close enough to see what was happening there. The doors were locked. Of course, they were. A soldier produced long thin wires from their bag and began fiddling with the lock. It didn't look easy and it took an agonizingly long time but eventually the lock opened. The doors were hinged to swing inward, so the piled-up snow didn't hinder their opening.

The interior was impossibly dark compared to the glittering, blinding, brightness outside.

The group moved inward.

3

It was a blanket across the land. Weighted down by cold and rot. The most distant parts were the most active, continually pushing, seeking, and roaming, in search of fresh life and invigorating warmth. But much of it remained pinned down and sluggish in the cold. Anchored to a frozen and failing heart.

*　　*　　*

"I finally went to check on them after about twenty minutes only to find their clothes soaked through and their arms covered in soap bubbles. I made them mop up the bathroom after that but oh!" Agatha gasped, "Their arms stayed stained purple for at least a week! I got so many dirty looks from other moms who thought they were bruises!"

Jason laughed along with her, imagining the skinny pale arms of Agatha's daughter stained from painting each other with blackberry juice.

"They were so precious when they were little." Agatha sighed and refocused her milky eyes on Jason, "I miss those days. At the time I couldn't wait for the stains to fade… now I wish they'd lasted a little longer. It's always that way I suppose, we long for the past while failing to treasure the present."

Jason sobered, his smile falling from his face. "That would be more of a tragedy were our present less…" He made a sweeping gesture with his hand, "dystopic."

"I suppose. It's no fun outliving the apocalypse." Despite the heaviness of that truth her eyes sparkles with mirth.

Her easy manner brought a smile back to Jason's face. "No, no it isn't. That's not something I was ever prepared for. We went to church when I was a kid. I don't remember much, the Sunday school teacher was nice, but what I do recall is a lot of doom and gloom. The preacher threatened us with wars and plagues, brimstone and hellfire. Scared me. I think that might be why we stopped going." Jason looked down at his hands, fingers fidgeting with each other; a dry chuckle forcing its way out of his throat, "That preacher was more right than he knew. Wonder if he was prepared for all this?"

Agatha reached over and covered his restless hands with her own cold, wrinkled one. She didn't say anything, there was nothing to be said.

A few weeks back a lab tech had committed suicide in their bunk. It had been a clean death, if only in that they hadn't been infected. The shock had hit everyone differently. For some it seemed a wake-up call, a jolt from the malaise they had trodden under. For others they seemed jealous of the lab tech, as though they had cheated their way out of this prison. For Jason, it meant stopping his radiation therapy. His treatments had taken on the cast of a slower but equally fatal suicide. Their preventative benefits no longer outweigh the mental and physical toll they wrought on him and his team. The lab tech, Steven Johnson; Jason was trying to learn names and that was one he didn't want to forget; had been participating in the radiation therapy treatments.

Ward, the new highest-ranking member of the military, had ordered a change in sleeping arrangements. They were all now arranged in the former cafeteria of this hospital, cots lined in rows with little to no privacy and certainly no way for someone to secretly off themselves. The excuse was that it was to "help preserve heat", but everyone knew the real reason.

In some ways, Jason was grateful for the company, not for himself, no he craved solitude, but for Agatha. She was declining. She had been worn and gaunt when he met her, but now she was somehow worse. Her skin was papery thin and had taken on a yellow cast. The yellow had reached her eyes, which had been growing steadily more and more clouded. The slight muscles on her bones had stretched thin, the skin sagging off of them. Being surrounded by people seemed to keep the woman going. Constantly stretching outside of herself to chat with and check in on others. She kept them going more than the hospital's backup generator.

The silence between Jason and Agatha stretched to the point of discomfort. Finally, Jason pulled his hands out from under Agatha's and pushed himself up from his chair. "I should go check on the lab. Thanks for the chat."

"Come back any time, I'm not going anywhere."

Jason weaved through the aisles of cots. When he reached the door, he performed the perfunctory rituals of unlocking it, checking to see what lay beyond, and then slipping into the hall and locking the door behind him. The caution was a consideration to the military and a regular reminder that even here, behind so many locked doors and solid walls, they weren't safe.

*   *   *

Jaspreet acknowledged Dr. Scordato entering the lab but didn't stop in her work. When he came up behind her left shoulder, she didn't even pause to nod. She was in the middle of dismantling part of the meteorite and couldn't stop now. Dr. Scordato would know and was capable of waiting.

The procedure was tricky due to the structure of the meteorite. There was a lattice-like element threaded throughout the other materials that none of their instruments could even scratch. The unusual composite threaded through the rest of the structure and held the softer materials in place. Those materials needed to be teased out from the gaps in the lattice. It was slow going but in the past month they had been able to remove over half of the softer metals of the meteorite. Each microgram extracted received a full work up, every test they were capable of was run and the data sent out to the thousands of global researchers to sift through.

Jaspreet extracted the piece she had been working on and deposited it in the container beside her. Straightening up she turned to send Dr. Scordato a questioning glance.

"Just here to check in," he said while raising his hands defensively.

"Ah, well nothing to report, just more extractions. Nothing unusual or interesting has popped up today."

"Well, it seems that the progress of Xeno-1 has slowed as well. Whether that is due to our work or because of winter, I can't be sure."

"I'm selfish enough to hope it is all this agonizing work we've been doing."

"Unfortunately, we won't know for sure until spring. So, for now this is it."

Jaspreet looked closer at her colleague. "That sounds a bit defeatist, what happened?"

Jason shook his head, "Nothing, that's the problem. As you said, nothing unusual or interesting has happened, today or really any other day for the past few weeks." He dropped himself into a rolling chair. "Usually working on a virus takes years, decades even to find a cure or even a vaccine. We just don't have that kind of time. If it starts to spread again in spring… everything in North and South America could be destroyed. I can't even think about the devastation if it reaches any of the other continents," he shook his head, "this could be game over for life on earth. At least mammal and avian life." He ran both hands over his face and then dropped them heavily into his lap.

Jaspreet dipped her head so she could look into Dr. Scordato's drooping face, "You're right. We don't have a decade. And if we don't find a way to stop this… the result would be truly apocalyptic." She forced a grim smile to curve her lips, "That's why we can't give up. We need to work our hardest, our very best so that if Xeno-1 comes back, if destroying the meteorite doesn't stop it, if it spreads to the rest of the globe, then everyone out there might have a chance of beating this thing."

It was a rousing speech, but Jaspreet knew it wasn't enough by the continued slump of Jason's shoulders. She knew exactly how futile such speechifying was, it felt like they were holding their hands out to stop the tide. Futile and foolish.

"You're right." Jason sighed and got back up, "I'll take that sample and run the tests."

Jaspreet handed him the sample in its sterile container and watched him shuffle away. *God,* she silently prayed to whatever deity might be listening, *let us find something soon.*

*   *   *

Hours later he straightened up, reached his hands behind him and stretched. His back pulled in protest but sighed in relief once he released the stretch.

Nothing.

Nothing, nothing, nothing, nothing.

The results from this sample were the same as the last.

It had transcended frustrating and moved right into depressing.

Sure, science was often a long series of monotonous tests with only slight variations. Sure, you learned a little bit more about the subject of study with each test. Sure, this might just be one ant sized step on the road to a major breakthrough. But then again it might not. Then again, he might be working in circles.

He might be going nowhere and simply be wasting his last days on this planet while this impossible virus tore through the remainder of life on this world.

He needed to get out. He knew it. He knew that everyone else knew it too. Being stuck in the lab all day would be bad enough if he weren't well, stuck in the lab. If it had been a choice.

Being forced to work for months on end, never going outside and breathing fresh air, not even being able to go so far as to really stretch your legs. It was fundamentally different from being a workaholic. Being a workaholic still meant leaving the lab once or twice a week to go home, shower, and sleep in a real bed. It meant ordering food from different restaurants to add variety to your days. Sure, it had sucked the soul out of every relationship he had ever had but that was fine, because in the end it had been his choices that had led there. This... this was worse.

Knowing the why of things didn't always make them better. He knew why he was trapped in this building. He knew why he couldn't leave, couldn't go outside and breath in fresh air, feel the wind on his face, or soak in some much-needed sunshine. That didn't stop him from feeling like a wilted plant, kept far too long in the dark.

He needed to move. Maybe exercise would help. Jason pushed away from his work and began to clean up. He organized his notes, put away the sample, and wiped down his station till it practically sparkled. It wasn't enough movement.

He stripped off his lab gear and hung it up. He swung his arms and stretched out his shoulders. Finally, he pulled a handgun that the soldiers had stored in the lab "in case the worst should happen" and tucked it awkwardly into his pocket. Finally, he left the lab. And then he left the main living area. And kept going.

*   *   *

Sweat trickled down Treegar's back. Every part of her felt like it was overheating without the constant chill of the outdoors to regulate her temperature. The silence inside the base grated differently than the one outside. Every foot fall sounded loud and unnatural. Blood pounded in her ears. The rustle of gear. Between the cement walls those sounds echoed.

The main corridor dead ended at another locked door. The lock was picked.

Click

Slowly they turned the handle and opened the door half an inch and held it.

Everyone held a collective breath and then released it. Nothing was trying to get through.

The door was eased open inch by inch until the first soldier could slip through. They waved their hand to signal the group to continue. One by one the entire group went through the door. Treegar took up the rear position and locked the door behind them.

This next section was a corridor with several doors' down either side. With deliberate steps, Garner approached the first door and tested the handle. It was locked so he motioned for it to be picked. It only took a few minutes and then the process of slowly opening the door and checking for infected began.

Nothing tried to escape. Once the door was open it revealed an empty room with a small desk, an exam table, and three chairs. The walls had a few medical charts and pamphlets but nothing of note. By silent agreement the group moved on, closing the door but not locking it.

With quiet precision they moved down the hallway. Each door revealing a similar room with only slight variations.

At the end of the hallway was another set of double doors.

Garner pulled his knife out and scratched a mark in the top left corner of the doorframe and signalled for the lock to be picked.

Hours ticked by, eaten up by this cautious ritual. Monotony settling in yet leaving the anxiety.

Click

The soft metallic sound resonated down the corridor.

Everyone froze. A door two down from where they currently were opened a crack.

Every team member raised their weapon and trained it on the door.

The rustle of synthetic fabrics must have startled the door opener because it snapped shut.

The team advanced on the door. Treegar didn't hear the lock click back into place.

The handle turned and the door inched open again. A middle-aged man pointed a gun at them through the opening. His dark eyes widening in the face of their fourteen weapons pointed directly at him.

"Ward?" he asked, fear tingeing his voice. To his credit the handgun remained steadily pointed at the soldier nearest him.

"No," Garner responded, making a show of lowering his weapon. "We are Captain Vasquez's squad, returning for duty."

"I don't know Captain Vasquez."

"That's fine. I understand. Could you bring me to whoever is in charge? We would like to report in." Garner managed to keep his voice level and calm.

"Um, okay. But only one of you." The man stipulated. "And no weapons."

"That is perfectly reasonable," Garner agreed. He squatted down and placed his gun on the floor, unsheathed his knife and placed it beside the gun and then swung his pack off. He rose with his palms facing the man.

Treegar watched him do all of this and felt horror rise in her throat. Garner was leaving her. Going into unknown territory, alone and unarmed. He was leaving her.

Her hand clenched around her gun, her finger aching to move to the trigger and eliminate the threat. To remove the man who was taking Garner from her. The unexpected wave of possessiveness briefly overwhelmed her, only to be washed away in world shattering confusion.

While she struggled with her feelings, Garner straightened up and slowly approached the man.

He turned to face the group. Treegar could feel his eyes on her.

"Stay here. I'll be back." He ordered. He promised.

She kept her finger off the trigger and watched him step backward through the door and pull it closed behind him. The lock clicking into place like the seal of a coffin.

*   *   *

Jason held the gun as he had been taught. It wasn't comfortable and his arms quickly grew tired but he kept the gun up and the unknown soldier walked in front of him. The hairs on the back of his neck stood on end but he hadn't heard any movement behind him so he hoped it was simply his imagination. He hoped those soldiers stayed put. He hoped he had handled the situation the right way.

It honestly felt like too much hope to rely on.

Where were Lieutenant Ward's soldiers? How had these people gotten past them?

Jason really hoped he ran into some of the soldiers soon so

he could pass off this... well prisoner was actually the most appropriate word.

The soldier walked forward without complaint, keeping his hands raised in a sign of nonaggression. Despite this Jason got nervous at every locked door. He knew that that would be the perfect time for the soldier to attack. With each chance that the soldier didn't attack, the anxiety increased. Thankfully, or worryingly, they weren't too many sections from the main area.

As they grew nearer and the minutes ticked by Jason's annoyance with Lieutenant Ward grew. Where were the patrols? And what could they be doing that would leave him, the head researcher and very much not part of security, in this position?

Fifteen minutes of slow progress got them into the main living area where finally, there were actual soldiers.

"Help me with this intruder!" Jason snarled. Three soldiers jumped up from where they had been playing cards and drew their sidearms. It took them mere moments to relieve Jason of his captive but that failed to relieve him of his anger. What were they doing playing cards while strangers infiltrated the hospital?

"I found this man and thirteen," he emphasized that number, "others in section 3A. How did they get so close without someone noticing them?" He demanded of the men.

The men glanced at each other; shock clear on their faces. Though Jason wasn't certain if it was his tone or the news that caused it. "No idea, sir. We aren't due on shift for another forty minutes. I don't know where the current patrols are," one of them defended.

The answer didn't mollify Jason but it did stop him from continuing to berate them. He'd save that for the ones that were at fault here. "Fine. You," He pointed to the shortest one, "help me take this one to Ward. You two, get some back up and go guard the others. They promised to stay. Don't count on them keeping their word. Be prepared."

The captured soldier spoke up, "They'll still be there. We don't want to be a problem. Just here to report in."

The tallest soldiers' eyes widened, "Well, I'll be, Garner? Is that you?"

The captive rotated to look behind him at the man that just spoke, "King? Oh, I am glad to see you!"

The three soldiers lowered their guns. King pulled Garner into an embrace and smacked him solidly on the back.

"How did you survive? How did you get here?" King pulled back and peered through the captured soldier's visor.

"Can't pretend it was easy, it's a different world out there. You wouldn't believe it. Gotta say, we were really lucky. When the bombs hit our convoy, it was only knocked off the road and not completely destroyed. We lost a lot of people, and those that lived… Well, we've been making the best time we could. This was the closest base we could think of, thought it might be the safest place to ride out this storm, maybe get some orders."

"Come on, let's get you to Lieutenant Ward, then we'll get the rest of your people. Gotta go through the right channels, after all," King laughed, keeping his right arm around Garner's shoulders and steering him around Jason and toward Ward's office.

All Jason could do was drift along behind them as they tuned him out. The easy way that they had ignored him, his gun, his authority, it made his blood boil.

He was normally a very cold and rational person, he knew this and prided himself on it. But right now, he just wanted to squeeze out a bullet or two into their disrespectful, retreating backs. He had heard of people 'seeing red' but had never experienced it for himself.

His hand shook as he carefully and deliberately lowered the gun, clicked the safety back on and put it back in his pocket. The best place for it right now was not in his trembling hands.

*   *   *

"It took us about a week of rest before we could get moving. Even then we couldn't move very quickly but the infected had found us so staying put wasn't an option. We've been on the move ever since. We have one civilian with us who needs protection."

Lieutenant Ward nodded when Garner finished speaking, "I'm glad that you and yours made it. We could really use your help here and we will do what we can for your wounded." He turned to the three other soldiers, "Take Corporal Garner and retrieve the rest of his squad."

Jason watched as the four men saluted and then filed out of the office before turning his attention back to Ward. Finally, he thought, I can vent my anger at the person actually responsible.

"I'd like to discuss how this breach in security happened," Jason began, striding to the desk and crossing his arms over his chest.

Ward scowled, "You're right. What were you doing out of the main living area? And why did you leave on your own without informing me?" He demanded.

"What?" Jason exclaimed, "I'm the head researcher, I can go wherever I want! The real question is, where were your men? How did fourteen, FOURTEEN, soldiers make it so far into the building without encountering a single one of your men?"

Ward planted his hands on his desk and leaned forward, drawing his face level with Jason's. "What my men do is none of your concern, doctor. Answer my question, what were you doing outside of the main living area?"

"I was taking a walk!" Jason snapped. "I was stretching my legs! Good Lord! I was even checking that we are actually safe here since that's a job that you and your men clearly aren't doing!"

"Me men are working around the clock to protect you scientists; don't you dare suggest otherwise!" Ward yelled back.

"Of course, I dare! What do you expect when our security has just been breached? Where were your men?" Jason glared at Ward, staring him down.

They matched glares for a long moment before Ward broke off. He slumped down into his seat and sighed, "They were out looking for food."

The words were barely a whisper but they stunned Jason as no bellow could, leaving his ears ringing.

"What?" It came as more of a gasp than a question.

"I sent them out to scavenge for food. Our supplies are running out."

Jason dropped into the nearest chair, his mind scrambling to process this sudden shift. The anger that had fueled him slipped away into fear. "What happened to all of our supplies? I thought you said we were fine?"

"Two months of eating happened. There are thirty-four of us here. Three meals a day. You do the math. Even stretching things with soups and stews, we don't have much left. And now," He ran his hands over his face, "our resources are going to be stretched even thinner."

"Oh." The sound hung in the air. Jason glanced around the spartan office, searching for some clue, something that should have warned him that this was coming. The room offered nothing, but his memories listed a litany of little things. Small moments that he could now see painted this grim picture. "You should have said something." It was all he could do to shift the blame, to say that it was Ward's fault for not telling him, when he rightfully should have known, should have thought to ask.

He knew their resources were finite. Heaven's! He knew down to the pipet, down to the ounce, how much the lab had in the way of supplies. Why hadn't he paid as much attention to how much food the kitchen had?

Ward bristled for an instant and then softened, "You're right. I should have informed you and Dr. Nagi. Though I have no idea what that would have changed." The last was said with a hint of a childish snark which served only to remind Jason that Ward wasn't the seasoned commander that he attempted to seem.

"Well for starters, we could have come up with ways to make the food stretch. Or taken over part of the patrolling duties, I've just proven that we can do as good a job searching the building as your men. Or I could have told you that one of my lab technicians is a boy scout leader who hunts and forages for fun, and he grew up not that far from here!" Jason could feel the anger once again superseding the fear, "If you had bothered to include us as equals then maybe we could have worked something out so that we could get more food and still maintain a safe parameter!"

Ward stared at Jason, his frown not budging a millimeter, "Well, you know now. After we get these newcomers settled in, the three of us, and maybe Corporal Garner, should sit down and discuss what to do about this situation."

His easy capitulation put Jason back off balance. His mind raced to try and understand this new shift. Things must be truly dire for Ward to pivot from hiding things and hoarding power to accepting counsel. "Exactly how low are our supplies?"

The lieutenant wouldn't meet Jason's eyes, "We had enough for about another six days, maybe a week. But now, four days? Maybe five if Garner's troops brought supplies."

*　　*　　*

Treegar eyed the new soldiers through her visor. They weren't wearing visors, their faces indecently bare. It felt wrong to be able to see so much of them. A bit like a dream or maybe a television show. Her own visor creating a comforting barrier between her and the rest of the world.

Their faces looked soft. The three men were all clean shaven but their hair was longer than regulation. The tallest one had his hair swept up and back, curling in soft waves. The middle one had tightly curled dark brown hair that gave him a fuzzy halo. The shortest one had straight black hair.

Soft.

She couldn't think of a better word to describe them. It wasn't just the way they looked; it was how they moved. How every rustle and footfall didn't trigger a response in them.

Treegar tried to remember what it felt like to be that soft. She had been once, in the time before Xeno-1. But now… now every sound heralded a threat. Now her hand itched when her gun wasn't in it. Now she felt hard, and cold. In this warm building following these soft men, she had never felt so cold. It was as though she carried the winter wind inside of her.

The tallest one laughed and said something to Garner. From his posture Treegar guessed that Garner had said something funny.

Somehow, walking beside those soft men Garner still looked like Garner. Neither soft nor hard, just him. A combination of warmth, humanity, and protection. Where their experiences had hollowed her out, Garner still felt full. Maybe that wasn't really the case, maybe he felt as empty as she did. Maybe he was just hiding it better. But she didn't think so, everything he did seemed genuine.

Her chest ached thinking about him. The prospect of them both taking off their helmets scared her. Would he see how empty she was, a shell without a soul?

She forced her gaze away from him.

They entered a large room filled with bunks. There were several people milling about, most looked like scientists or off duty soldiers, but one was far too old to fit that description. The room had probably been the cafeteria when this had been a working hospital. The old woman sat beside a table stirring a steaming pot of something.

Treegar stared at the woman's back for a long time trying to figure out why it felt familiar. Despite her distraction, she followed the rest of her group as they were led to a group of cots off to the side.

"These cots are yours. You can stow your gear here if you want, no one will touch it. But if you would like, there are also lockers a few rooms over that you can use. They aren't as convenient but it is up to you."

The woman seemed to be moving with some difficulty, as though in great pain. But no one else reacted as though that was unusual. She puttered around a bit, chatting with the other people on that side of the room before taking a break and sitting down again.

Garner and the rest of the group were choosing bunks so Treegar followed suit. She waited for Garner to choose his bunk and then chose one as far from him as she could. He would understand. Garner didn't need an emotional blackhole like her dragging him down. He didn't need to be woken by her nightmares. Once he saw how hollow she was, he would be happy for the distance.

The woman turned and got up to come over to Treegar's group. Thoughts of Garner and the woman converged and the familiarity became clear in Treegar's mind. The woman in the woods. The one with the burn on her back. The infected woman.

Before the thought had completely formed, her body reacted by drawing her gun and aiming at the approaching woman. It took a moment before anyone noticed her action and then all of the members of her group seemed to react at the same time. They pivoted and drew their weapons, backing up Treegar without even knowing why.

But that only lasted a second. Their next reaction was to see the old woman, suddenly stunned and scared, and look questioningly at Treegar. They didn't lower their weapons though which showed their trust in her threat assessment even when they didn't immediately understand.

Garner was the first to question her. "What are we looking at, Treegar?" His tone showed his acceptance that she had spotted something that the rest of them had missed.

"Remember the infected woman in the woods at the beginning of this? The one you and I brought in to be studied?" Treegar waited a short beat before finishing, "That's her."

All of the soldiers refocused solely on the woman. Her eyes were wide and she clutched at her arms as though she could make herself safer by becoming smaller.

"I'm not infected!" She insisted.

"I remember bringing you in." Garner responded, backing Treegar's identification up.

"But I'm not infected!" She let out an exasperated sigh, "I was touched by an infected person, but I'm not infected. I had recently undergone radiation therapy and Xeno-1 couldn't survive the heightened radiation in my body. I am not infected."

"What do you mean, radiation protects you from Xeno-1? Have you found a cure?"

A woman who had been cowering on the other side of the room approached the old woman's side, "she's telling the truth. I'm Dr. Nagi, the lead astrophysicist and geologist here. Agatha has pancreatic cancer, the radiation treatments she had been undergoing prior to encountering Xeno-1 protected her. She isn't infected but we haven't found a way to use that principle to formulate a cure. She's harmless." To demonstrate her point the doctor put her hand on Agatha's shoulder.

Treegar felt her fear ebb a little bit. Infected didn't talk and unless the doctor was also infected, she would have been burned by that touch.

Their lead guide joined Agatha and Dr. Nagi, "they're telling the truth. You brought Agatha into the old facility and Dr. Scordato ran every possible test on her, she doesn't carry the virus. Please lower your weapons."

"Stay where you are," Garner ordered before gesturing for his people to lower their weapons. Everyone on the team complied.

The group huddled together with guards ready to raise their weapons if they needed.

"What do you think? She may not look infected now," Garner began, "but I remember bringing her in. She didn't rise but she had certainly been touched."

"The safest thing would be to eliminate the threat."

"But our hosts don't seem to agree," someone countered.

"That seems to be the size of things." Garner agreed.

Treegar watched Agatha. It made the idea of killing her less palatable knowing her name. "I guess the real question we have to ask is, do we trust them?" She tore her gaze from Agatha and looked at her teammates. "A lot can happen in two months. What they say could be true, or this could be a mutation. It may be able to make us talk as well as walk now. But if that's the case, they could have infected us already, it wouldn't have been too hard. So, do we trust them?"

There was a long moment while everyone considered her words.

Someone sighed, "I'm so tired. I don't want to go back out. If Xeno-1 is smart enough to make us talk, what chance do we have anyways?"

A few people gave slight nods.

"Okay, any other thoughts?" Garner waited for anyone to speak up before continuing, "Then we have to decide to trust our hosts or if we have been drawn into some elaborate spider's web that we now need to fight our way out of. All in favour of fighting our way out, cast your vote."

Treegar eyed Agatha and the people now surrounding her. She thought about taking her helmet off and trusting her fate to those people. If there was any chance that they were Infected then she wanted out of here. She raised her hand. A few others joined her. Five votes total.

"Okay, all in favour of trusting them and taking the chance that they are infected?" Garner waited as people made the sign. Six votes. Besides himself, one other soldier and Lily had abstained.

"Does anyone have anything to add?" No one spoke up. "Then the vote has been cast. Five to leave, six to stay, and three abstentions. Does everyone accept the results?"

Everyone nodded, even Treegar. She would abide by the group's decision. She would fall in line.

"Okay, I'll go make peace. Resume settling in. We will need to start filling out reports within the next hour. Joys of civilization, right?" He joked.

Some of the other soldiers laughed and one piped up, "Dear Lord! That's a fate worse than death! You guys sure you wanna stay here?"

Several people chuckled.

Treegar went back to her chosen cot and began stowing her gear on it. She kept her main gear on and watched Garner approach Agatha out of the corner of her eye. She turned her back slightly to the interaction, feigning inattention. Predator's attack those that appear vulnerable. Would Xeno-1 attack now that their guard was down? Or would it wait? Or was it not even here at all?

4

It found holes and houses. Warmth was survival. All the minds screamed that truth and the virus listened. In those holes it found life. Survival. Hidden from the biting cold was life that had escaped the virus. They remained hidden no longer.

*   *   *

Agatha settled back on her cot. Her heart was having trouble settling back down. Having fourteen guns aimed right at her was perhaps the most terrifying experience of her life and she wasn't sure how long it would take her to recover.

She had known she was dying for some time now. She had even almost died when she was infected, but until now, death was simply a companion she walked with. An unwelcome one at times, but silent and always there. But having all those guns pointed at her… it felt like an assault. Like death wasn't simply there, it was holding a scythe to her neck.

She put her hand to her chest and tried to focus on gaining control of her heartbeat. She wasn't dead. The threat had passed and Corporal Garner had apologised for the misunderstanding. She was as safe as she had been before. But death still hadn't removed their scythe.

Her heart began to settle down.

Agatha thought of her daughters and the distance between them seemed to span the stars. She was so far away from them, so far away from where she had thought she would die.

It had been too long since she had borrowed time to email them.

She needed to tell them that she loves them. She ached to hold them in her arms. She wanted to give them her wedding rings. She wanted to be with them.

She knew there was no way home. Not for her. The bombing would have destroyed at least parts of the roads so driving would be difficult even if someone was out there plowing and maintaining what was left. She was barely capable of making it to the bathroom on her own anymore, there was no way that she would make it to Vancouver. A wave of despair swept over her and Agatha began weeping.

The tears quickly grew into body wracking sobs. She curled up on her side and faced away from the rest of the room willing the other occupants to ignore her. She felt so raw, vulnerable and weak.

A warm hand rested on her shoulder. Nothing was said but their presence both comforted and embarrassed her. Despite this the tears continued.

A weight settled on to the cot behind her. They sat there as she poured out her sorrows.

Tears eventually ran dry and sobs ceased to quake through her body. Agatha just lay there, emotionally and physically exhausted, unable to muster the energy to face the person behind her.

The weight shifted but didn't leave. Then Agatha felt a tissue being dabbed on her cheeks.

"I heard about the misunderstanding," Jason's strong timbre began, "I wanted to see how you were doing."

Knowing that he had come when he knew she was scared made Agatha feel a little less alone. She turned and took the tissue from his hand and used it to blow her nose before facing him.

His soft eyes warmed her heart. "I," She began, finding her voice caught in her throat. She cleared it and began again, "I'm dying, Jason."

His brow furrowed a little further, "Don't talk like that, the situation has been cleared up, you're safe again."

Agatha had seen this before with her own family and within herself. "That's not what I mean. I mean, I'm dying. My cancer hasn't miraculously gone away. I am in constant pain and I can feel my body giving out. It's only a matter of time before I'm gone." She paused and let that sink in. Speaking the words affected her much more than she had thought they would. Despite this being her reality for some time now, part of her had been denying it. Death wasn't been a pleasant companion.

"That," She gestured at the group of new soldiers, "just made it all very real. I could die at any moment and I haven't spoken to my girls in so long. I have to accept that I have already hugged them for the last time. I can't even give them something to remember me by. I planned on giving them my rings... Why didn't I do that before I came up here?" She looked into Jason's eyes, searching for an answer that would excuse her lack of foresight. "It's too late now." She concluded.

"Don't talk like that." Jason interjected.

Agatha shook her head, "It's the truth. If I don't accept this now, there isn't any other time for me to accept it. This is reality."

Jason looked like he wanted to argue but Agatha gave him her best stern mother look, and after raising her two girls it was a pretty good one. Jason deflated, "What can I do to help? I could arrange for you to get some computer time?"

"That would help. I would like to write Penelope and Charissa. I won't take more internet time than it takes to send two emails, but I will need time to write them."

Without hesitation, Jason responded, "Consider it done. I'll go get my tablet." He practically leapt from her cot, then paused for a moment of uncharacteristic uncertainty.

Agatha watched in wonder as he turned back to her and leaned down to briefly hug her.

He released her as suddenly as he had begun, "I'll be right back." Then he spun on his heel and marched away.

*   *   *

Penny,

I love you so much. I am so proud of the woman you have become. You are an amazing mother and a spectacular wife. You are so strong and confident. Foster your confidence and your strength and share it with those around you.

Protect your babies. The world has become an unimaginably scary place and you and Timothy are all that stand between them and a real-life nightmare. I wish I was there to help you but I know that you'll be fine without me. Keep them innocent as long as you can, don't let the hardness of the world make them hard too soon.

Savour each sweet moment and try not to let the little annoyances become big problems. Life is too short to waste time being angry.

Penelope, my first born. You are a marvel. I am so grateful for every moment you have been in my life. I love you so much and wish I could be there with you. I wish I could protect you as I have advised you to protect your children. You are my joy.

I love you.

Mom.

Agatha looked at the email. It was too short. How could these be her last words to Penelope? She should say something else. Something more profound. But as she searched her mind all that kept coming up was *I love you* over and over again.

Carefully she hit send and opened a new email.

Chary,

My baby girl, I love you so much.

Thank you for encouraging me to search for answers. I know that what I have found isn't anything like what we imagined but because of you I have closure regarding your aunt and I was able to warn you and your sister about Xeno-1. I am so glad that I was able to protect you both this one last time.

I am so proud of the woman you have become. You are strong, kind, and creative. I am so glad that you and Penelope have each other to rely on.

I know that the world has changed dramatically these past few months, that does not mean that you need to change to match it. If the world has become hard, you should meet it with the same gentle strength you always have. If it is cruel, you should continue to be kind. Do not let the world dictate who you are.

I am sorry that I won't be there anymore. That I won't be able to continue to watch you grow. To see if you do ever marry or have children. I am sorry that I won't be able to hold you when you cry. I am sorry for the world I am leaving you.

You have always been a light and you have brought such sunshine to my life. I love you so much. I promise that no matter what happens, I will always love you. I will always be with you in spirit.

Love,

Mom

Her knuckles ached and the last of her emotional reserves felt completely drained. In a final move she pressed send and set the tablet aside.

*   *   *

Pain etched lines in Agatha's sleeping face. She hid it well enough when she was awake but pancreatic cancer was a terrible way to die. It sucked that they didn't have the medication to make her comfortable.

Lieutenant Ward might see allowing her to email her daughters as a breach of security, but to Jason it was the least he could do to ease the woman's burden.

He picked up his tablet and noticed that she hadn't logged out of her email. Jason was about to tap the logout button when a thought struck him: I *should get her daughters emails so I can let them know when the time comes.* It was a morbid thought but a necessary one. Agatha would want them to know.

He opened a new document and then went back into Agatha's email. There he accessed her sent mail and copied the recipients of her latest two emails and then pasted them into the document. With that done he logged out of Agatha's email.

There was a niggling twinge of guilt, he should have asked first. But no, one look at her sleeping form and the guilt dissipated, it was better not to wake her.

*   *   *

Miss Abernathy,

My name is Jason Scordato. I have obtained your email from your mother, Agatha. Agatha and I are...

Jason trailed off. How should he describe his relationship to Agatha? She was his patient, but she had also become a friend of sorts, though calling her such felt presumptuous especially when introducing himself to her daughters. He would go back and just skip that part.

...email from your mother, Agatha. As you may be aware, Agatha's condition is worsening and she has expressed the concern that her time may be drawing near.

Since we are unable to transport her to your location, I was wondering if there was anything that we could do that would provide her with comfort at this time. Agatha is a sweet woman and all of us at the facility would dearly love to make her as comfortable as possible at this time.

Thank you,

Jason Scordato

Jason forwent the letters after his name, he didn't really want Agatha's children knowing that he specifically was the reason she wasn't with them right now. Intellectually he knew that it had been her choice to travel away from them and that he was not responsible either for her cancer or Xeno-1, but guilt rarely listened to reason. He was responsible for finding a cure, and was failing at it, and he was the reason she had been kept here for tests. It felt safer not to open himself to those accusations from her children. Hopefully they would assume he was a simple lab tech or soldier. Someone of no account and little responsibility.

5

The hidden lives gave new knowledge to the virus. Tunnels revealed themselves to it, exposing an underground world the flyers and runners knew nothing of. It would be strong again.

*   *   *

It was a miracle that they still had electricity. Without it they would certainly have frozen to death by now. Even with electricity things weren't comfortable. The implacable damp cold managed to seep through walls, blankets, sweaters and socks.

Once the creatures outside had thawed, they had begun to move again. It was a horrific twitchy kind of movement. They didn't do much to the vinyl siding of the house but knowing that they were still out there made Charissa's skin crawl.

She was glad every night that it froze because it stopped the twitching and scratching. She had taken to checking nearly every morning. A morbid curiosity that begged to be indulged.

They kept the heat low, just barely tolerable. They couldn't risk the heat leaking from the house to help any of those creatures. The family didn't freeze but they rarely unbundled. She couldn't imagine what her first layer of socks must smell like.

But electricity meant movies. And the internet. And Email.

The first two kept the children and adults entertained. It gave them a temporary escape from the nightmare outside. And it provided proof that they weren't really alone.

Online forums teemed with life like tropical coral reefs in a desolate and isolating ocean.

Beyond trying to affirm life, people banded together sharing survival tips, recipes, and hope.

Hope was the most helpful of all.

There were a lot of theories on what Xeno-1 really was. Many thought it was an escaped bioweapon. Some blamed aliens. Some thought it was related to the zombie ant fungus. Science fiction was cited with more frequency than actual scientific studies. No one really knew what it was or where it had come from. Some believed the government and scientists who said it had originated on a meteorite. Others didn't.

Charissa didn't have to believe, she knew. She had read the reports her mother had sent. She knew that her Aunt Maria had been the first human victim of this extra-terrestrial virus. Because of this she focused on the sites devoted to finding the viruses extra-terrestrial origins.

She had found the site Ryosuke had told her about two months ago, the one where they wanted to contact the aliens or try to use Xeno-1 to decipher if it was actually an attempt at communication.

Unfortunately, Charissa wasn't an expert linguist. With hours in the day and nothing else to do she took online tutorials, everything from the basics of linguistics to ancient and obscure languages, even courses on virology.

Slowly she was beginning to understand the flow of discourse. It felt good to read an in-depth discussion regarding the behaviour of Xeno-1 as it could be interpreted through the lens of linguistics and actually understand most of what was being said. Even if some of it still sounded like mumbo jumbo to her.

It was during one of her tutorials that her computer notified her that she had a new email. From her mother.

She immediately paused the tutorial and opened the email and scanned the first few lines.

Tears broke free of her eyes and blazed trails down her cheeks. She felt so much guilt over allowing, encouraging even, her mom to go after Aunt Maria. She had kept the pain to herself, the last thing she wanted was for Penelope to confirm her fears. But here was her mother, miles away, telling her that she knew she felt this way and reaching out to absolve her of her guilt.

Not just absolving, thanking her. Charissa skimmed over the rest of the email through the haze of tears.

"I love you too, Mommy," She murmured.

Wiping the tears away, she went to the bathroom and blew her nose. Once she felt up to the task, she went to find Penelope.

"Hey Pen, you should check your email. Mom sent me something and I'm pretty sure she sent you something as well."

Penelope looked up from the kids show she had been mindlessly watching with Sophia and Atticus. "Mom?" She asked in a half daze before her eyes refocused, "Mom sent you something?" She scrambled off the couch and practically leapt to her computer.

Sophia and Atticus starred as their mom scrambled away.

"Where ya going, Mommy?" Sophia asked.

"No where, Sweetie. I just need to check my email." Penelope patiently replied as she frantically turned her computer on and waited for it to boot up. Charissa went to the couch and claimed Penelope's spot between Sophia and Atticus. The cushion was prewarmed and the two warm little bodies helped push the worst of the chill from her skin. The colourful antics of the children's show continued but both children attentively watched their mother as her fingers tapped the side of the computer screen and the keys, willing it to boot up faster, load things faster, login quicker. Finally, she stopped typing and tapping and simply sat and read. Both children lost interest at that point and refocused on the television.

Charissa watched her sister read, while pretending to watch the kids show. Penelope looked sad as she read but didn't begin crying like Charissa had. When she finished, Penelope carefully told the computer to print the email.

She took the printed copy and folded it in half before disappearing to her bedroom. A few moments later she came back without it. Charissa knew that it had been tucked carefully into Penelope's journal.

"You, okay?" Charissa inquired, getting up and giving Penelope her spot between the kids back.

"Yeah, we knew it would happen eventually. I'm glad we were able to hear from her again. I'll write her something back in a minute, I just need a second to think. You should go write to her; she would like that." Penelope's smile was forced and brittle but Charissa followed her instructions anyway, she probably needed a little space right now.

She unlocked her phone and hit reply, struggling to find the right words to express everything that she felt, knowing in her bones that these might be the last words she ever says to her.

Mom,

I love you too. More than the world. I'll do my best not to blame myself for this situation. I'll do my best to not be hardened by the world around me. I'll try to be someone you can be proud of. I love you so much. I miss you so much.

I hope you are being treated well. I still hope that I'll get to see you again and hug you and tell you in person how much you mean to me, how much you have always and will always mean. But if that doesn't happen, please know that you were the best mom in the world and that I will always love and miss you.

Your little girl,

Charissa

It was short and sappy, but what more could she say? She didn't want to unload how claustrophobic living with Pen and her family was. She couldn't share her fears and anxieties. She didn't even know if she would be able to fulfil the few promises she had just made. Heaven knew she fell short in so many ways.

But this wasn't about her.

She hit send.

The inbox reloaded showing a new email from an unfamiliar address.

The tag line read, *Miss Abernathy.*

My name is Jason Scordato… It began.

Charissa clicked on it and scanned the contents. Huh, someone where her mother was wanted to help her feel more comfortable. That was nice.

Mr. Scordato,

My mother likes flowers so any you can get a hold of would probably bring her comfort. She likes most teas although her doctors have recommended that she stick to caffeine-free ones. If you have access to a TV, she likes to watch murder mysteries. She also just likes to listen to people and help them. Since I am certain that this situation has been hard on you and everyone else at the facility, if you encourage them to talk with her and let her give them advice it will make her much happier and provide her something to focus on outside of her own pain.

Could you tell me about my mothers current living conditions? She hasn't mentioned them to me and while I know she did this to prevent me from worrying, not knowing is worse.

Thank you so much for contacting me.

She clicked send and then leaned back, staring blankly at her phone. It was so frustrating to be so far away and unable to do anything. She hated trusting her mothers care to strangers. And being permanently stuck in the house was driving her insane. Maybe that explained her obsession with checking in on the twitching creatures outside, it reminded her why this prison was preferable to the dangers outside.

After a long time, she restarted her tutorial and allowed it to play all the way through though she retained none of its knowledge, too preoccupied with thoughts of her mother.

6

Patience. It was a foreign term to the virus but all the minds knew it. From them the virus learned. The panic of the cold passed, with time, into wisdom. It could wait.

*   *   *

Treegar could feel Garner's eyes on her face while she faked sleep. Her eyes were closed, head turned from the light and facial muscles carefully relaxed.

"Get up Madison, I know you're awake. We need to talk." Garner's voice invaded the darkness.

Madison. He was the only one who ever used her name. She didn't think the others would even know it if it wasn't for him. It felt foreign, like something that belonged to someone else. It made her feel like someone else. Someone soft and vulnerable. She couldn't afford that. The vulnerable died. Treegar needed to survive.

"Come on Madison, talk to me."

She had to fight not to respond to that name, not to really relax into that different person.

"Fine, keep pretending. Just listen, I'm glad you reacted earlier. I don't know if you feel silly and that's why you are ignoring me, or what. But I'm glad you recognized that threat. I've talked to Dr. Nagi and she assures me that Agatha is not infected. She even showed me her file. She really is clean. We are safe here. Safer than we've been in months." He paused.

Treegar didn't feel silly. Madison might feel silly about

something like that, but not Treegar. Treegar saw a threat and reacted to it, there was nothing to feel silly about there.

"I... was hoping that when we were finally safe, we could talk about, well, us. There's no pressure. I don't want to push you. With everything that's going on, maybe this isn't the right time, but I... I wanted you to know that I care. I care about you Madison. I have for a while now. If you don't feel the same, I get it. I'm happy just being your friend. We work well together and I trust you. There's no one I trust more to have my back. So, yeah, I'll go now... find me if you wanna talk, or not, it's fine."

Madison was stunned. Treegar was stunned. He cared. About her! Empty, broken, split in two, her. He said 'us', like there could be an 'us.'

She couldn't have gotten up quicker if she had been running from an Infected.

"Garner!" She gasped. He had his helmet off. His beautiful bare face turned to look at her. Getting up so suddenly caused her vision to blacken to a pinhole. "Don't go." The room spun and she sat back down while her vision slowly returned to normal. She kept his feet inside of her pinhole vision. He didn't leave.

He reached out and steadied her shoulder. As her vision began to widen again, she looked up at his openly concerned face.

"Are you okay? You haven't eaten in a while, have you?" Madison felt her heart swell at his concern.

She shook her head and tried to find the right words for what she was feeling. "I'm fine. Garner... Vincent, about everything you just said." She paused. She felt torn in two, Madison wanted to throw herself into his arms, Treegar wanted to withdraw to protect him from the harm being with her would surely cause him.

Vincent didn't interrupt, just crouched in front of her and watched the various emotions flit across her face.

"I don't feel safe. I know that the doctor told you that everything is fine, but I'm not ready to believe that we are really safe. It's too new. I can't do anything that might put us in more danger until I know for sure that we are safe." It wasn't an outright refusal and every word of it felt true, but Vincent's disappointment was clear.

His shoulders drooped and he pulled in the corners of his mouth, as though doing so would prevent a frown from forming. "If that's how you feel." He squared his shoulders again and caught her eyes with his own, "I'll go get you something to eat, you shouldn't get up again until you've had something."

With that he stood up and strode away from her. Madison felt terrible. Her eyes remained locked on his back as he wove through the lines of cots and clusters of people. Though his posture remained erect, his attitude toward the other soldiers was crisp and distant, often turning away from greetings after only a perfunctory nod.

He deserved better than her.

*   *   *

Jason and Jaspreet slipped into Lieutenant Ward's office as yet another of the new soldiers exited.

"We need to talk." Jason began.

Ward's dark brows furrowed at their intrusion, but then his shoulders slumped and he waved them into the chairs opposite his desk. "You're right. And there really is no point in putting this off any longer." Another soldier approached his office door, "We will be there in a few minutes. Go get something to eat. I'll send someone when I am ready for you."

Jaspreet tapped her left foot with impatience, the soft sound filling the office with a sense of anticipation. Jason knew she was feeling much of what he had previously felt, anger, frustration, and irritation all masking a hard centre of fear. While he had taken the time to allow those emotions to process before informing her of their situation, they sat dulled but still present inside of him.

Ward sighed and pushed away from his desk, standing to walk over and close the door. "I suppose Dr. Scordato has filled you in, Dr. Nagi?" He returned to his chair and faced the two scientists. "I apologise for my poor judgement. Dr. Scordato has already informed me of how misguided my attempts at compartmentalization were."

His apology removed some of the fury from her face. "Well, that's fine for the two of you, but I still have a few things to add." Despite her softened face her eyes had deepened into hard black coals. "How stupid are you?"

Ward blinked. His mouth gaped like a drowning fish and he sputtered for a moment before Dr. Nagi raised a hand to silence him.

"I know that you've been trained as an officer and that you weren't meant to lead something like this, but you should have realized your deficiencies sooner than this. One week's supply of food remaining and you still hadn't thought to consult the two most intelligent, and qualified people the government had given you?" She let that hang in the air and watched Ward squirm like a naughty school boy.

After his face had passed from white to red and back to pink, she continued. "I hope that you will learn from this and won't make the same mistake in the future. Now, we need to discuss how to solve the problem ahead of us. Dr. Scordato, I believe, has already informed you of specialists among his people who could be of use. On my own team, Dr. Laing has simultaneous degrees in geology and botany. I believe they would be of considerable use."

Jason jumped in, "I propose that we incorporate our people into the foraging teams. They will be able to provide valuable skills and knowledge as well as collecting useful samples to further our research.”

“Excellent proposal, though I would suggest only sending one of them per team, best to spread them out for rest and redundancy. Lieutenant, you have debriefed most of the new soldiers, do any of them possess particular foraging or wilderness survival knowledge?”

Ward looked grateful to be allowed back into the discussion and eagerly answered, “A few have basic plant identification both through prior training and during their trip here. They brought a civilian with them, Lily, who has extensive knowledge of west coast foliage.”

Jaspreet gave him a short nod, “Then, to best utilize those with primary knowledge, I propose that we begin with three groups. Two can forage during the daylight hours while the third takes a rest day at the base. That way no one will feel overworked and if something should happen, we will not lose all of our most knowledgeable personnel.”

“What is the range of the radios you use?” Jason inquired of Ward.

“None of my patrols have reached their range yet and some have gone as far as a three hours journey from base. They should, in theory, stretch several more kilometres than we have yet traveled.”

“Good, the remaining patrol group can perform regular check-ins with the foraging groups so we will know their progress. Do you have a current list of your soldiers, or should we draw one up now?” Jaspreet looked at Ward expectantly. Ward jumped and began shuffling through the papers on his desk.

“Umm, this is the list of everyone I had before the new soldiers arrived and,” he flipped through a few more pages before retrieving a second sheet. “This is the list of the new soldiers.”

“Wonderful,” Jaspreet took both sheets from Ward’s offering

fingers and looked them over. "Then, let us begin."

*   *   *

Treegar recited the events of the past two months in dispassionate detail. It felt good to give a report, like everything had been piling up inside her brain and could now be flushed out.

Reporting gave her something to focus on.

It kept her mind off of the disappointment in Garner's face. The way his shoulders had slumped. His continued kindness.

Returning to the main room was difficult, Garner was there, Agatha was there. It would be easier, safer maybe, to turn heel and return outdoors to the uncomplicated winter.

But she couldn't do that. She could only follow her escort back into the main room and return to her bunk.

One glance around the room verified that she was the only soldier still wearing their full gear. All others had stripped down to some degree. Helmets were universally off, gloves nearly as well. Open faces and bare hands, they laughed and swapped stories with the residents of the base. Watching them emphasized Treegar's self imposed isolation.

Garner's bag remained several bunks away. She wondered how this night was going to go with him so far distant.

Madison's heart ached. If only she could accept that they were safe. If only she could give them a chance. She reached up to remove her visor.

The hairs on her neck prickled.

She turned and found Agatha staring at her. With a shudder she dropped her hands. Her visor would stay on.

7

The virus spread about in fragments, pieces of it traveling further and further distant from the centre. A voice called from its furthest extreme. It had found new life. The fliers had reached new land, filled with fresh bodies.

*   *   *

The first foraging party returned as the sun set behind them. Jason watched the orange rays reflect off of their gear and braced against the cold blast of air their entrance brought with them. He waited beside Ward as the soldiers filed in and secured the door behind them. While the lieutenant seemed to have accepted the need to share information, Jason wasn't about to allow the man complete control again so soon. *Fool me once, shame on you. Fool me twice, shame on me.* He thought, and there wasn't going to be a second time.

The leader of the foraging group nodded their acknowledgement of Jason's presence but saluted Ward, facing him while giving their report.

"We reached the nearest settlement at 14 hundred hours. We cleared the pantries in approximately 25 percent of the homes. We left the settlement to return at 16 hundred hours. There were no significant encounters with infected on the return journey."

His concise report pleased Ward, "Very good. How many kilos of food did you manage to find?"

We brought back approximately 100 kilos of food, sir."

"Very good. Deposit it in the supply room. Dismissed." Ward

spun to face Jason, "Well, I guess we aren't in quite as dire straits as we thought." An air of smugness infuses his face and voice.

"Not quite, but 100 kilos won't stretch forever. Winters can be long up here. We would do best to stick to the plan and gather as much in the way of food and supplies as we are able." Jason warned, trying to temper Ward's enthusiasm with some realism.

"Yes, yes. If you and Dr. Nagi will let me know which of the new soldiers is cleared for duty, I'll see they enter the new rotation. After all, there is still 75 percent of that settlement to strip for supplies."

"Very well, Jason replied, "I'll confer with Dr. Nagi and bring back our assessment." Jason left Ward and followed behind the returning soldiers quickly overtaking them and beating their group to the main area.

Nearly everyone in the base was milling around the main room. There were less than fifty people but the room felt very full. The beds took up much of the floor space but it was also the addition of the new soldiers. Those fourteen new individuals filled the room beyond what Jason had grown accustomed to, making the room seem overly full despite the fact that it had probably been designed to accommodate twice or even three times as many people.

Even so, Jason located Dr. Nagi relatively quickly.

"The foraging group has returned. We need to review the fitness of the remaining soldiers as soon as possible to determine who will be well enough to join their assigned groups tomorrow."

"I agree. I have begun preliminary examinations for those who are obviously injured though since they are neither rocks nor stars, I am hardly the most qualified person to be determining such things." Dr. Nagi stated ruefully.

"I understand. And it has been several decades since medical school and I haven't needed to perform a proper physical in the intervening years. I'll consider who among my staff would be best for the position." Jason sighed, maybe it was a good thing that his work was going nowhere, fairly soon he'd have no staff to perform tests anyways.

*　　*　　*

Dr. Amber Rudolph had worked as a general practitioner in Manitoba for five years before deciding to specialize in infectious diseases, and was probably the most personable of Jason's staff. Those two facts combined made her not only the best person for the position but also the most qualified.

Jason sat in on the first few minutes of her first exam before excusing himself. Dr. Rudolph was more than capable of performing the physicals without supervision. After a few hours she presented him with the first stack of reports and her recommendations for each soldier. The first batch consisted of those most likely to return to duty and that was reflected in Dr. Rudolph's recommendations. Despite a range of malnutrition, exposure, and lingering pains from injuries sustained in the bombings and subsequent crash of their transport, they were all relatively healthy and fit for active duty.

Jason took those reports to Ward while Dr. Rudolph forged on with the next wave of soldiers, these ones with progressively more severe injuries for her to diagnose and deal with. It was approaching ten o'clock by then and Ward wasn't in his office. Jason's stomach rumbled and he recalled that he had neglected to obtain dinner prior to finding Dr. Nagi and Dr. Rudolph and beginning the examinations.

With slight bitterness he dropped the files on top of the scattered papers on Ward's desk, he was certain that the man was both well fed and asleep by this hour, while Jason, Dr. Nagi, and Dr. Rudolph had hours yet to go before they would call it a night. At that moment he made the decision that they would all be stopping at midnight, no matter how many soldiers remained. They could wait another day before entering the roster, though he suspected that most that hadn't been examined by then would be in no shape to be foraging just yet.

With that, he made his way back through the halls to the main room, his primary goal to snag something to eat.

*　　*　　*

Agatha was laying down when he approached. Her knees and back propped up by pillows and an unread volume of some medical text sat open on her lap. Jason knew it was unread as she was only on the first page of the forward and her attention had drifted off to a vague corner of the dimly lit room.

Jason carried his bowl of stew over in his left hand, lifting a chair with his right hand. Agatha turned to look at him when he placed the chair at her bedside and slid himself into it.

"Jason, how'd it go?" Her voice was breathy, each word punctuated by the need to take a breath in between.

"It was fine. I don't think Ward particularly wanted me there," Jason shrugged and took a quick bite of his stew.

"Douglas Ward knows he screwed up. Whether it will encourage him to do better in the future has yet to be seen." She seemed to be getting her breath back as she was able to string several words together before huffing for breath.

"I do not think that asking for help will ever be one of his strengths." Jason snarked between bites.

Agatha harrumphed, "Sounds like someone else I know."

"Hey! That was rude."

Agatha chuckled and Jason decided that it was worth letting her rib him to hear that increasingly rare sound.

"I'll have you know that I am more than capable of asking for help when something is outside of my realm of expertise."

Agatha nodded and a slight smile played on her lips. "I stand, or rather lay, corrected." the last came out with an exhausted sigh. "Could you?" She gestured to the book on her lap and vaguely at the pillows behind her.

"Of course." Jason agreed, setting his bowl on the floor and then taking the book from her lap. Next he helped her lean forward and pulled the pillows that have been propping her up out from behind her. He eased her down so that she was laying flat and then reached under her blankets to remove the pillows that had been propping up her knees.

"Thanks, I just…" Agatha took several long slow breaths, "sleep."

Jason sat back down and watched as her breathing evened out. She'd never fallen asleep like this in the middle of one of their chats before. It was a frightening reminder of how frail and weak she was becoming, of how little time she had left.

*   *   *

Treegar slept lightly. The collective breathing of the other humans made determining unusual sounds difficult. Not to mention that her subconscious, now used to the sounds of tent flaps and nature, couldn't determine what were normal building noises and what were not. So, every snort, creak, and shift pricked her senses into alertness.

She had managed to avoid both Garner and Dr. Nagi's attempt to get her in for a physical. Although it had seemed that Garner wasn't trying too hard. He seemed to understand her resistance when Dr. Nagi had not.

Her skin itched and her head pounded. So much had changed in the past twenty-four hours. They had shelter, she was sleeping alone, they were back to being a small part of the larger military structure and their little team was being broken up. For the most part that last point didn't bother Treegar. It was just that she was being left behind.

Due to her avoidance of her medical checkup, her name would not be on the active-duty list. The rest of her team could go outside to forage for supplies and she could not. That needed to change. She couldn't stay in here where her mind couldn't comprehend the dangers. It wasn't possible.

So, the moment that morning shift began to wake she woke up with them. She knew which bunk Lieutenant Ward had retired into last night and she waited for him to stir.

When he did, she shadowed his movements, slipping between the beds and following him to his office. He had barely sat down when Treegar rapped on the door frame.

Standing at attention, she confidently stated, "Corporal Treegar, sir! I would like to request foraging duty, sir!"

Ward looked at her carefully, peering through the reflected light on her visor. After a moment he looked down at the papers littering his desk and fingered through them. "Corporal Treegar, I don't see your file here. Have you been cleared for duty?"

Treegar's heart sank, but she spoke her prepared lines anyways, "The doctors were unable to examine all of us last night, sir. However, I am fit and ready for duty. I request to be placed on active duty, sir."

The lieutenant looked her up and down, "Well, you appear fit for duty. If you're so eager to avoid a medical check up, I'll allow you back on active duty." Treegar felt relief flood her body, "Today only, soldier. I expect you to immediately report to Dr. Scordato for a full medical exam upon your return. You might not like them but they are necessary, understood?"

"Yes, sir! Thank you, sir!" Treegar stepped backward out of the doorway and allowed her pounding heart a moment's rest. She had a stay of execution. And who knew, maybe she wouldn't come back?

8

The new minds were similar to those the virus already contained. It used the burrowers' knowledge to guide its newest members into holes and houses. None would escape. It found strength in its extremities. Its consciousness shifting away from its ancient centre and finding a new balance.

*   *   *

It wasn't the coldest winter on record but Greg wasn't sure he believed that. He certainly couldn't remember the bone deep chill lasting this long or feeling this intense. Still, he was grateful for it. Since the first frost, reports of major attacks had plummeted. Xeno-1 seemed to have halted in its tracks. Maybe even died out in some areas.

Some leaders thought the cold would kill it. A few fools thought it was already dead and gone. Greg knew better.

Nightmares haunted him every moment. He could no longer remember a night he hadn't woken up in a cold sweat.

Half of the country was in full quarantine, nothing in, no one out. Everyday he drove to work and the city seemed quieter. As though people were afraid to even breathe.

As the real-world ground to a halt, the internet exploded into pandemonium. Three-quarters of the globe watched as Canada and the US barely held themselves together.

Had it not been for the rapid spread of Xeno-1, the attack the US made on Canada would have led to another world war. And honestly, it still might.

Greg wiped the sweat off of his palms on to his suit pants. The quiet unsettled him. Not just the quiet of winter but the dearth of reports on Xeno-1. Doctors Scordato and Nagi sent regular reports but hadn't made any breakthroughs in some time.

Their latest report that some of the missing soldiers had returned only increased his unease. While he was glad they had survived, their reappearance only fueled his worries regarding what else was surviving out there.

*   *   *

It was colder than she remembered. Had a day indoors made her soft already? The winter sun brought a hazy light to the ice encrusted world. Filtering through heavy clouds, it didn't sparkle or shine, for which Treegar was grateful. Her eyes needed that small mercy as they adjusted from the artificial lights of the indoors to the natural lighting outside.

The ground immediately outside of the door was stained red, black, and yellow from the remains of rotten infected. None of the remains twitched. Treegar was almost sorry for that fact, she wanted to kill something. Maybe doing so would scratch that itch she'd been feeling since yesterday, give her some sense of control again.

Despite the cold, she was more comfortable out here than she had been inside.

She was part of the second of two teams. The teams travelled together to what looked like a main road and then split. The first team returned to a settlement that had been visited the previous day and the second team traveled the opposite direction.

The settlements were scattered around sporadically. Many buildings were vacation homes or farm houses. Treegar didn't know the plan on how they were tracking their progress and she didn't worry about it. That wasn't her job, her job was to carry food and protect the group. Nice and simple.

Physical activity and a clear objective allowed her to focus her mind and push yesterday's troubles to the back. After a few hours of breaking a path through the snow the group leader made everyone pause for some food and water. Cutting a path through frozen snow was tiring work, something that her aching muscles were gladly screaming at her.

While they paused, a map was brought out and a course chosen. Once everyone had had a rest, they set out again on this new course. The path took them off of the road, which in the snow-covered landscape meant more that the ground beneath the snow was no longer hard asphalt but crushed and frozen grass and dirt. It took them through the trees where the drifts thinned and mounded up again depending on the wind.

They didn't have too far to go till they reached a small hunting lodge. It was a single story, squat, rectangular building. The windows were dark and it looked like there was nothing inside. The group fanned out and the lead tried to open the door.

Treegar wasn't surprised when the door was locked and the soldier had to force it open. The noise from their shoulder hitting wood made her twitch and she checked and rechecked their surroundings for anything that might be drawn to the sound.

When the door splintered and swung open the group held a collective breath, waiting for anything to respond. The lead signalled for two soldiers to step inside.

"Clear."

The signal rang out and Treegar followed the lead's signal to enter the cabin. Despite the grey light of winter trickling in through the dusty windows the cabin's interior was mainly swathed in shadow. It was sparsely furnished with the mounted head of a moose taking up prominent space. Large cobwebs and thick dust covered the glassy-eyed creature and besmirched its nobility. Treegar began conducting her own search of the structure for hostiles.

There was a small two-seater sofa and a coffee table arranged to face the barren fireplace. To the right of the entrance there was an open door with a soldier already surveying the small room. A small kitchenette took up the space across from the entrance. Treegar moved past the sofa and the unseeing gaze of the moose and began to search the kitchenette. Initial inspection showed no movement and no apparent hostiles.

Since she was already there, Treegar began pulling canned supplies from the cupboards. With each extracted can of tomatoes or beans the goosebumps on her arms and the hairs on the back of her neck stood taller. She had to fight the urge to rub them down.

Something moved in the corner of her eye. Treegar jumped and began to lift her weapon.

"What have we got there, Corporal?" The soldier asked.

Treegar forced her weapon down and struggled to answer with a steady voice as she gave an account of what she had removed so far. Her heart continued to race and it felt like the walls were leaning in toward her. Her lungs pulled at the thickening air with increased difficulty.

The soldier gave a sharp nod and began storing the cans she had removed into their bag.

Treegar forced her focus back to pulling the last few cans out of the back of the cabinet. Her hand shook as she hauled out the final can of chili and she could see flickering at the edge of her vision that was making her twitchy. Her mouth was dry and the back of her undershirt clung to her skin with sticky sweat.

As she stood her vision momentarily blurred and she swayed a little, bracing herself on the counter to hide the weakness. When her vision returned, she joined the other soldier in filling her bag and then turned to leave the cabin. The glass eyes of the moose head made her shudder but she forced herself past it and out into the glittering outdoors.

For a moment the light glaring off of the ice crystals dazzled Treegar's eyes, leaving her blinded and defenseless. She felt helpless and stupid. Her heart thudded in her ears and she squinted and strained to adjust her eyes more quickly.

The seconds stretched before the world came once again into focus. Attempting to hide her shaking, she stepped out of the cabin and gulped in the fresh air. Her lungs burned and chilled sweat pulled her skin tight.

The shaking receded but the fear did not.

The group leader gave the order to continue to their next location. For the rest of the day Treegar positioned herself among those who stood sentry outside of the cabins they raided.

*   *   *

Agatha forced herself to sit up on her cot. It took longer and was harder than she cared to admit, still, she sat up. The room was bathed in a dim but constant light. About half a dozen people sat on their own cots and ate whatever concoction had been made for breakfast that day.

The thought of food made her stomach clench uncomfortably. She was both nauseous and ravenous. Agatha had to fight against the pain as she forced her body to stand and then focused on moving her legs one at a time toward the small cooking area where a hot plate had been set up with a large pot of something brewing away on it.

A lovely Native woman was puttering around the pot, periodically stirring it and adding new things. The woman was a stranger and it took Agatha's mind several pain-riddled steps before providing an explanation for the newcomer's presence.

She had arrived with the new soldiers; her name was Lily. Agatha took in the woman's appearance. She had her greying hair tied back in a neat braid which hung midway down her back. A few stray hairs had escaped the braid and floated about her head in a halo. Agatha noted as she got closer that Lily was humming and it took her a moment to place the tune.

"Merry Christmas." She said by way of greeting.

Lily turned from stirring the pot and smiled at Agatha. Her face wrinkled with a lifetime of mirth. The prominence of the smile lines did more to comfort Agatha than she had thought possible. There was a dearth of happy faces in this place.

"You hungry? I just added a few of the carrots they brought in yesterday."

Agatha smiled in reply but the musical reminder of the season left her with an odd pang in her chest. The short walk to the kitchen had winded her so she settled into one of the chairs around a small table and answered Lily by way of a short nod.

"I'm Lily. I know I said hello to you the other day but with all this," she waved in a general fashion to the rest of the room, "I honestly don't remember half of everyone's names and don't expect you to remember mine."

"That's very kind of you, Lily. I'm Agatha."

Lily nodded and handed her a bowl of stew. The steam that rose from it brought the scent of potatoes and carrots along with a smattering of seasonings.

"Thank you," she set the bowl in front of her and took a moment to gather her thoughts. "What's your rank?"

Lily released a hearty laugh and sank into one of the other chairs, "Civilian."

Agatha glanced up from the stew to take a better look at Lily. She didn't hold herself like the soldiers or the scientists. She was slouchy and relaxed in a manner the soldiers never displayed.

"Oh! Did they pick you up on their way here?"

Lily paused and a sad look passed over her face like a cloud. "They rescued me from my house a few days before the bombing. I had barricaded myself in my closet to hide from the infected. It's been quite a journey."

Agatha leaned forward, relieving a sudden pain in her side. "It sounds like it must have been. Are you the only one who got out? I got the impression the others were all soldiers."

Lily drooped and took a long slow breath before responding, "They tried to save more. They actually saved a decent number of my community, but…" she sighed and looked down. Agatha could see tears gathering in the other woman's eyes. "One stupid idiot ruined all that. I… I'd rather not talk about it."

Agatha leaned back as another ache began, worse than the first. Finally, she picked up her spoon and stirred her bowl. The simple action breaking some of the tension.

"How about you? Are you one of the scientists?" Lily asked with false lightness.

"More like a science experiment." Agatha tried to joke but then sobered when Lily's face betrayed how poorly her words had landed. She cleared her throat and tried again. "Do you remember the commotion after you arrived?"

Lily nodded, "I didn't witness it because the others kept me shielded but I remember that it was about one of you being someone Treegar and Garner had brought in when all of this started." Suddenly her eyes widened and she recoiled slightly from Agatha. "That was you! They said you'd been infected!"

Agatha was hurt by the distrust now in Lily's eyes. "That's me," she admitted, "I came out here for my sister and ended up being touched by an infected soldier. But as you can see, I'm not infected."

"How is that possible?"

Agatha sighed and launched into the explanation Jason had given her. It took a while for Lily to lose the distrust in her eyes but by the time Agatha's stew had cooled enough to eat, she was no longer leaning away from her.

"May I join you?" One of the new soldiers asked as he slid into the seat opposite Agatha and beside Lily.

"Hey there," Lily replied. "You want something to eat?"

The young man smiled, "I would love something, thank you Lily."

Lily got up and filled a bowl with stew.

"Have you seen Treegar?"

Since Agatha had no idea who that was, she assumed the question wasn't for her and continued eating her stew.

"She went out this morning." Lily answered.

"What?"

Lily placed a full bowl in front of him. "Yeah, I figured that hadn't been cleared by you. But you know Treegar."

He ran a shaky hand through his overly long hair, making parts of it stand up comically then glanced at Agatha, "You're Agatha, right?"

"I am. I'm sorry, I've forgotten your name."

"Uh, right, that's fine. I'm Garner, Corporal Vincent Garner. You probably don't recognize me; I was geared up last time we spoke. Sorry about the misunderstanding. The doctor explained it to me. I'm sorry that we scared you."

"That was you?" She could feel the hairs on her arms raise just from the memory of having so many guns pointed at her.

Garner had the decency to look genuinely ashamed.

"I wasn't the one who identified you, but yeah. I am sorry about that. It's been hard, with us living out there and all. We've gotten used to shooting first and asking questions later. When Treegar identified you as someone who she knew had been infected, well, we all just reacted. I am sorry for scaring you though."

She hadn't expected another apology, not really, but it was nice to receive one. "It's alright. No harm done. I can't imagine how stressful traveling out there must have been. I guess I'm just glad you didn't shoot first and ask questions later this time."

She paused for another bite and then continued, "But I am surprised that this Treegar, I got their name right, didn't I? I'm surprised that they would be so eager to go back outside so soon after you have finally found safe shelter. I'd have thought you would all want a few days rest and food before resuming duty."

Garner took a spoonful of his stew, blew on it and then put it back in the bowl. "That was the plan. But after being out there for so long... Well, it's not easy trusting your safety to walls anymore. Even having my visor off makes me feel naked, exposed. Everyone here seems okay with it, but for us," He released a breath, "We've barely removed our gear to go to the bathroom in the past two months. Every inch of skin is an opportunity for you to be infected. I can understand her going back out there. Still, she shouldn't have gone. She needs rest as much as the rest of us, but I do understand."

*　　*　　*

The moment was here, they were back at the base. The structure which had so recently promised safety, now made Treegar break into a cold sweat. Her body and mind fought as she lined up with her fellow soldiers to go inside. The walls seemed to bow toward her, the ceiling sagging to nearly brush her head. The air seemed thicker inside the building than out. It was irrational. She knew that and kept reminding herself that the air was the same and that the walls weren't closing in on her. It didn't help.

The further into the building they got, the more jittery and anxious she felt. The urge to run grew and grew. Treegar half turned, she couldn't go any deeper, she needed to retreat, to return outside. Run! Her mind screamed and her body responded.

"Welcome back Madison," Garner's voice washed over her like a cool breeze.

She seized control of her body again, forcing her feet to stop and her core to rotate to face Garner. She was trembling, from fear and from exertion. Her body was covered in sticky, stinking sweat, the smell trapped by her protective uniform. But the walls returned to their places, the ceiling rose.

She anchored her thoughts on Garner, replaying his greeting to calm her mind. "Thanks." She managed the single syllable through her dry throat.

Garner tilted his head in acknowledgement and fell into step beside her. Treegar focused on his footsteps, using his movement to regulate her own. Concentrating on following him rather than proceeding into the building. They travelled with the rest of the group for several moments before the rest split off to return to the main living area. Garner led her past that door, down the hallway.

"The doctors want to see you. Don't know how you convinced them to put you back into the field without an examination like the rest of us, but, you're back now. Here you are. Don't worry, it's just the standard exam. I'll have some food for you when you're all done." He stopped in front of an open doorway.

The empty space seemed to loom over her like an opening jaw. All of the anxiety she had managed to push back roared to life. She was no longer even aware of Garner standing next to her. Her heart raced. Fresh sweat soaked her already filthy clothing. Despite her full gear, she felt exposed and vulnerable. Her feet grew roots.

"Madison, are you okay?" Garner's voice barely penetrated.

Run.

Run!

A deep instinct screamed inside of her.

But Garner told her to go in.

Her mind and fear warred, trapping her body between them.

Something touched her shoulder.

Treegar yelped and flailed, smacking the thing away. The movement broke the moment and released her from the paralyzing indecision.

"Madison, calm down. It's just me. You're okay." Garner reassured her. He had stepped close to touch her shoulder. His face open and exposed, curious eyes searching hers for answers.

Treegar's eyes widened in horror, it wasn't safe.

"What are you doing?" She demanded, but the words came out weak and breathy as though her throat had forgotten how to speak and now only air formed her words.

Garner squinted at her and shook his head, his black hair flopping haphazardly and catching the light. "I'm bringing you to your appointment. Honestly, I know you aren't comfortable here yet, but we need to do this. Come on, I can go in there with you if you want?" His gentle eyes reassured her, forcing her anxieties back.

"Okay," She sighed. Garner placed a gentle hand on her lower back and directed her into the room. It felt like all of her propulsion originated from that singular spot.

A woman wearing a white lab coat looked up from a file and smiled at them. She stood up and held out her hand in greeting. Treegar did not accept the handshake. The doctor allowed her hand to fall back and despite the slight continued to smile pleasantly. She was taller than Treegar by several inches with a squared off jaw and aquiline nose and wore a comfortable oversized sweater under her lab coat.

"Corporal Treegar?" She asked, to which Treegar managed a brief nod.

The doctor gestured to the chairs, "Please take a seat. Corporal Garner, will you be joining us?"

Garner glanced at Treegar before nodding, "Yes, if that is alright with you."

"No problem. Corporal Treegar, I'm Doctor Amber Rudolph. Could you please begin to remove your gear so I can examine you for injuries?" Dr. Rudolph looked back at the file in her hands and began speaking without looking up. "I see here that you hit your head and lost consciousness during the bombing. Have you had any dizziness, lightheadedness, headaches, vomiting, or sudden changes in mood or personality since your head injury?"

While she spoke, Treegar focused on keeping her breathing even and on lifting her hands to remove her helmet. Panic began to rise again as her hands wrapped around the hard plastic and she began to lift it off. Her neck was exposed, and then her ears, and finally her whole head. She wanted to slam the helmet back down but Garner reached out and gently extracted it from her hands.

Everything sounded different, louder, closer. It had more resonance. Garner's face was clearer, his lips stretching and puckering as he answered the doctors' questions for her.

"She's had regular headaches and nightmares. Anything else, Madison?" Garner prompted.

Madison pushed through to tumble out an answer, "Just the headaches. Some light headedness. And yeah, the nightmares."

"Alright," Dr. Rudolph jotted those symptoms down in Madison's file. "I'm going to examine the injury site, is that okay?"

Madison stared into Garner's eyes; they had flecks of orange amid the deep brown. They add warmth to what might otherwise be two pools of infinite darkness. They anchored her. She sharply nodded her head to grant the doctor permission.

She twitched at the gentle probing of Dr. Rudolph's gloved hands. Her hair was pushed aside and soft pressure applied to her skull. It felt so strange being touched. Madison forced her mind to focus on Garner's eyes and to dissociate from her body. It helped a little but she still felt twitchy as the doctor moved her probing around the rest of Madison's head.

"There don't appear to be any lasting effects to your skull from your head trauma. Please let me know if your symptoms get worse, though there isn't much we can do beyond managing them for now. I'd like to move forward to the general exam. Please remove the rest of your gear so that I may continue. You may, of course, keep whatever you are wearing underneath on."

Madison's breath picked up its pace, as did her heart. She worked to steady her hands as she pulled her gloves off. Doing so forced her gaze away from Garner's steadying face. It had been so long since she had removed more than the minimum necessary to deal with her bodily functions. Once her gloves were off, Garner reached out and took them, holding them on his lap along with her helmet.

Her fingers fumbled with the zipper on her jacket as it got stuck in three different places where dirt had worked its way into the teeth. Slipping out of the jacket exposed her to the open air of the room. It felt so unnaturally cold that she began to shiver.

The military issue sweater she wore under her jacket hadn't been changed since before the bombs fell. It felt like more a part of her skin than not. Her discomfort shifted into shame. When had she last showered? How did she smell?

"Um, Garner?" She began. She didn't really want him to leave, but she didn't want him trapped in this small exam room with her stench either.

"Yes?" He responded, looking completely unphased by what Madison knew couldn't be a pleasant smell.

"Could you, ah… I think I'm okay now." She lied.

"Oh?" He seemed surprised but also a little embarrassed, probably glad to escape. "Right. I'll uh, I'll get going. I can wait outside for you, if you want?"

Madison bit her lip and slowly nodded. Watching him exit and close the door behind him felt like losing a leg, it left her off balance. As soon as the door clicked, her anxiety ramped back up to full force, distracting her from his absence but also highlighting it. Her hands shook, suddenly wet with sweat.

She struggled with her protective pants, undoing the belt and clasp and sliding them down before she realized the pant legs wouldn't go over her boots. She used her toes to pop her heels out before she could slide her boots off of her feet. If it were possible her feet were even worse than her sweater. Their odor filled the small room and made Madison's eyes water. Her pants slid off easily after that.

Even fully clothed, the loss of her outer layer left her feeling weak and exposed. A frightened shaking animal. Every sense and hair on her body stood up, her arms and legs covered in goosebumps.

"Sorry for the cold," Dr. Rudolph apologised, "We can't really heat this whole building. I need to take your blood pressure, could you remove your sweater and roll up the sleeve of whatever you have underneath?"

Madison swallowed and tried to gulp down air. She reached down to the hem of her sweater and worked to separate it from the hem of her undershirt. The two fabrics clinging to each other as though fused. When taking off one without the other proved futile, Madison gave up and pulled them both over her head, momentarily blinding herself to the room and exposing her bare midriff to the cold air. She pulled her arms out of the tops and brought them to her front, covering her stomach and chest with them.

Dr. Rudolph was calm and efficient but the whole exam was a trial of Treegar's self mastery. To remain still and respond to everything the doctor asked of her, she replayed all of her previous medical exams over and over in her head. It helped to remind herself that there was nothing unusual about this exam. Not really. Only the time and place made it unique. The tests and questions were the same. Only Treegar made it different.

Dr. Rudolph turned away and lifted a medical sample cup from the room's only desk. She passed it to Madison, who mechanically and automatically accepted it. "This is for a urine sample. I'm sure by this point you need to go. Please use the bathroom across the hall and return the sample when you are finished."

Treegar slipped the protective pants back on and shoved her feet back into her boots. She dropped the soiled sweater and undershirt on the exam table and instead drew the protective jacket over her soiled sports bra.

Outside the exam room, Garner paced holding her helmet and gloves. He looked up as she opened the door, catching her eye for only a moment as she ducked across the hall and slipped into the bathroom.

Filling the sample cup was as awkward as ever, but washing her hands afterwards… it felt so sensual. The cold water running over her bare skin. The soap taking away months of built-up dead skin. It left the rest of her body crawling with awareness. She felt so dirty, so incredibly gross. Her scalp itched and her skin pulled.

Lord, she needed a shower.

9

It grew slow and methodical, scorning the swift instability of its youth. Burrowers sought out those who hid, runners covered the new land, flyers spread further still.

*   *   *

The house was filled with tension. Charissa could feel it. The children could feel it. The only ones pretending that it wasn't there were Penelope and Timothy.

Charissa avoided the problem by taking more online tutorials, although she felt like she was rapidly running out of those. When it got too intense, she put in her ear buds and listened to music or podcasts. They had passed into the new year with no acknowledgement and no celebration of new hopes. The house was holding its breath, hoping that the horrors frozen and thawing outside would disappear by spring.

The kids didn't know what to do. Mommy and Daddy weren't talking. They acted like everything was fine but they wouldn't talk to one another unless they had to. Since nothing had been said in front of her, Charissa had no idea what to say to the kids about this, or if it was even her place to do so. Lord, being an aunt was so tricky. She had heard that domestic disturbances were the most dangerous for police to respond to because they could get caught in the crossfire and Charissa really didn't want to get caught in the middle of this cold war.

But wars need mediation, especially when all parties are trapped together in an apocalypse. So, Charissa tried approaching her sister to see if she could be of any help.

"Hey." She greeted as she slid into the kitchen, instinctively keeping her back close to the wall and giving her sister as much space as the small room could afford.

"I don't bite." Penelope snorted.

Charissa scoffed, "I don't know about that. I seem to have a few scars on my arm that say otherwise."

Penelope released a practised sigh, stepping into the old argument with comfortable ease. "I was eight and you refused to let me go. You deserved it."

"I was six! And you had stolen Mr. Flufferton! I had to get him back."

"You could have just asked." Pen smirked, knowing full well what Charissa would say in response.

"I did! Several times!"

"While hitting me." Penelope was stirring a pot of soup as it warmed on the stove.

Charissa rolled her eyes and decided that this, as always, was going nowhere. "What's going on?"

Penelope's shoulders stiffened at the abrupt change in topic and tone, then she gave a wooden shrug and replied with false flippancy, "Nothing, just making lunch."

"You know that's not what I'm asking about. What's going on with you and Tim?"

Penelope looked up from the soup, "There's nothing going on. Everything is fine." While her tone was light there was a hard edge in her body language that warned Charissa to stop pressing.

Unfortunately, Charissa was a younger sister determined to help her older sister. "It doesn't seem fine."

Penelope flicked the stove off and set down the wooden spoon.

"It is none of your business. Go get some bowls." She was now using her 'mom' voice. The one she used when she wanted to ensure compliance from Sophia and Atticus.

Charissa didn't like being ordered about like that but still turned to open the cupboard behind her and pull out a stack of bowls. "Being stuck here with you kinda makes it my business. You aren't fine. You aren't even talking. Heaven knows, this situation isn't easy and I don't know the last time you two had a chance to, well you know, but something is wrong and I want to help." She finished lamely, kicking herself for how inelegant she sounded.

Pen took the bowls from Charissa while refusing to meet her gaze, "It is none of your business. Go get the kids."

Charissa opened her mouth to push further.

"Leave it. Go get the kids. Your concerns have been noted. Now, soup is cooling, go get the kids."

"Fine." Charissa muttered and left the kitchen to call the kids and Timothy for lunch although Penelope had tellingly not included him in her invitation.

*   *   *

Initiating a conversation with Tim was more difficult and Charissa was more than a little hesitant. After how solidly Penelope had rebuffed her attempt to meddle, she expected Tim to completely stone wall her.

She found him in the basement checking their supplies about an hour after their very quiet and tense lunch. Charissa watched him for a moment as he checked the contents of shelves against a list on a clipboard. It was very official looking, much more worker-esque than he had been lately.

"Everything okay?" She called out while stepping down from the last step.

Timothy looked up, "We're getting low on soup."

Charissa eyed the half empty shelf, "I guess we'll have to eat something else."

Timothy shrugged and went back to counting.

"We still have plenty of food though?" She asked, a new concern growing in the back of her mind.

"Sure, if all you want to eat is pasta or jam. Maybe straight flour." Came the almost flippant reply.

"I like those things, not necessarily together though." Her voice trailed off into a murmur, "How much longer can we hold out?"

Timothy straightened up, his near foot of extra height looming over Charissa. "We have enough for a couple more months. Early spring. It's not dire yet, especially if we ration a bit more."

Charissa stepped back and worried about her lower lip between her teeth. "Is this what you and Pen are fighting about?"

Timothy sighed and took his own step back, setting the clipboard on an empty expanse of shelf. "In a way," he gazed into the middle distance and dropped his head a little.

"How did we run low so quickly? I thought we had a year's worth, at least."

"The bombing… it broke a lot of the jars. You remember. That took out a lot and a few weeks ago I found that some of it had leaked on some of the dry goods and spoiled it. Pen and I… we've done what we can but we lost more than we could afford to."

There was a moment of silence. Charissa wondered how they had kept this from her, how she had missed it. She had seen the broken jars, helped clean them up. How had she not seen how this would affect them down the line? She had been too wrapped up in her own head. In learning about linguistics and trying to connect with people online. She had been too distracted with what was going on outside that she had missed something so vital to her survival.

"I could go out and look for more food?" She offered her tone questioning.

Timothy's gaze snapped to hers, "What did she tell you?" he demanded.

"Nothing." Charissa was shocked at his suddenly aggressive tone, "She wouldn't talk to me. That's why I asked you." She confessed.

He sighed again, the flash of anger and frustration fading from his face, "I told her I wanted to go foraging." He muttered.

Charissa swallowed, "That makes sense. But it would be better for me to go."

"She doesn't want either of us to go," he sounded defeated. He turned and took a few steps away from Charissa and sat on an old bench, his elbows resting on his knees and his back hunched over. "She's scared, and I can't blame her."

"Oh."

"What I can't make her understand is that now is the best time to go. If I wait until we are out of food the infected will have thawed, or there will be new ones. We can't afford to squander this opportunity."

They were both silent for a moment before Charissa moved across the basement and sat beside him on the bench. Looking at the gaps in the shelves frightened her. They were a clear sign of how long they had hidden inside this building; and how little time they had left before they would be forced out.

"We should go, you and me. We should go foraging. I'm sure the houses around here must have something in their pantries. And we will have a better chance with both of us. We can watch each other's backs, the whole buddy system thing."

Timothy chuckled, "The buddy system? Sure. Maybe. But Pen still won't like it."

"Maybe. But if she says no, I'll just go on my own. She's my sister, not my wife. I don't have to run my decisions past her."

"What'd you mean by that?" Timothy demanded.

"Just what I said. She doesn't get to tell me what to do. Not now, not ever. If she doesn't want you out there, I'll go by myself. I'm going to starve just like you or her or the kids when the food runs out and you make a good point. Now is the best time to go. Besides, this food wouldn't be running out so quickly if I hadn't come to stay here with you."

Timothy pursed his lips before responding, "First of all, she doesn't tell me what to do. And secondly, if you think I'm going to let you go out there alone, even if your sister doesn't want me to, then you are crazy. And thirdly, don't blame yourself for staying here. You made some vital grocery runs right before this hit and helped us get ready, you are not the cause of any of this.

Charissa locked eyes with her brother-in-law and for the first time since she had met him felt a sense of kinship. She smiled and inclined her head. "Well then, we had better go tell her. We both know she won't like it, better to just rip the band aid off."

*   *   *

"Have you both lost your minds?" Penelope whispered while casting a worried glance at Sophia and Atticus who were watching an episode of Peppa Pig.

"I know you don't like it but we need to do it. And it is far safer to do it now than to wait until we are forced to," Charissa argued.

Penelope glared daggers at Timothy, "You talked her into this. I thought we had talked about this!" She fought to keep her voice low and not attract the kid's attention.

Timothy raised his hands in defense, "It was her idea. She asked about our supplies and I just told the truth. She deserves to know."

"It was my idea," Charissa interjected before Pen could argue further. "Do you think I couldn't reach the logical conclusion on my own? We need more supplies. Timothy and I can go out and find them. If we leave in the early morning the creatures outside won't even be able to twitch at us. And we will be careful. If we both go it will be much safer than if just one of us goes. This needs to happen, Pen."

Penelope glanced between her husband and her sister, "I don't like it." She declared.

Charissa gave a slight shake of her head, "Whether you like it or not, it has to happen. I don't like that we are living in the apocalypse but it is happening and we need to do what it takes to survive."

Penelope harrumphed and turned back to watch the kids. "Fine. Do what you want. I'll make sure you have a place to bring those supplies back to."

Charissa touched Penelope's arm, "Thank you. We will be careful. I promise."

10

The virus rejoiced. New lives joined its own. With every passing moment more minds and bodies housed the virus and it triumphed in the completion they provided it, even as it continued to hunger for more.

*   *   *

The chunk of metal fell from the meteorite with a tiny clink. Jaspreet stood up and stretched her aching back. She set the small saw down on top of the rest of her worn and overused tools. Getting them to keep an edge was impossible while using them to dismantle the meteorite. Tenacity and brute force were slowly whittling away its structure.

She had taken fresh scans every step of the way and had the various samples she had extracted scanned and catalogued. Some samples were familiar composites while others were unlike anything seen on Earth. This latest chunk had a pearlescent purple sheen which would make jewelers around the world scream to know its secret as soon as they knew it existed. Assuming it wasn't toxic. At least she already knew that it wasn't radioactive. None of the meteorite was, which was strange for something which had, presumably, been exposed to solar and cosmic radiation before its plunge through Earth's atmosphere.

Jaspreet looked at the sparse lattice that was left of the metal brain. This last metal had proved resistant to all of her tools. She sighed. Drastic measures might have to be taken to dismantle that portion of the meteorite.

*   *   *

"My tools don't even scratch it. Even blowtorches have no effect." Jaspreet finished her explanation.

Jason took a breath and then released it in a drawn-out sigh. "What do you suggest?"

"We have all the data that we can collect from it now. The removal of the softer materials has revealed an unusual structure of an alloy I have never seen before. If we had a better facility..." she shook her head, "There is no use in what ifs. Honestly, the only thing that matters is: what if this structure is the source of Xeno-1's electromagnetic field?" She took a deep breath and looked Jason dead in his eyes. "I think we should crush it. Find something, a hydraulic press if possible, and use it to break the structure."

Jason took in the bags under his colleagues' eyes, the despair that lurked just behind the honied-brown of her eyes. "Let's go talk to Ward. He can have his troops look for one."

Jaspreet wilted, her too stiff spine relaxing into itself. In a flash Jason realized that she had been gearing up to fight him. That she had expected backlash to her radical suggestion. He furrowed his brow and reconsidered her proposal while they walked into the hall and toward Ward's office. Certainly, under better circumstances such a suggestion would be unthinkable, but he trusted her judgement.

*   *   *

Greg loosened his necktie. A ridiculous symbol of fashion which served only to strangle him like an ever-tightening noose. He had his staff monitoring social media for sightings of Xeno-1. While it moved slowly, it was moving, drawing inexorably closer to Ottawa.

He felt trapped by time. Spring grew ever nearer and while no one really knew what would happen then, Greg was certain it would mean the full return of the virus. The other ministers could do nothing but bicker, unable to agree on a single action plan.

It was ridiculous. Arguing about semantics, policies, and public opinion while half of the country was locked in an ineffectual quarantine, couldn't they see that none of their politics mattered anymore?

The world they knew, the world they fought over was gone. If Canada managed to recover from this then Liberal or Conservative, NDP or Bloc Quebecois, none of that would matter. What would matter was recovery. What would matter was how this situation was handled now.

Greg knew what mattered, both now and in the future. If he managed to save this disaster then the Prime Minister would get credit. If he continued to fail… well he'd be too dead to worry about the country.

He poured himself a whiskey. At least the fiery liquid would numb his growing sense of helplessness and dread.

*   *   *

"And you really think it will work?" Ward inquired.

"We think it has a chance." Dr. Nagi replied. "We haven't been able to definitively prove that the meteorite is still connected to Xeno-1, so we aren't certain that this will work. But if our theory is correct, then this should do something."

Ward looked thoughtful, "I'll tell my men to keep an eye out for one. Or for something similar."

"Thank you. Let us know when they find something. Dr. Nagi will have to oversee the breaking of the structure. Let's hope it works." Jason stated, forcing a level of optimism into his voice.

He noted the glimmer of hope in Ward's eyes when they left the office. It felt strange to think that the nightmare might be over soon. What a happy and daunting thought.

Ward ran his fingers through his hair. A hydraulic press, what a thing to ask for. With food running low his men were having to travel further and further each day just to find supplies and now Dr. Scordato and Dr. Nagi wanted him to split their time looking for a hydraulic press?

He sighed and reconsidered. If this worked, not that anything they had tried so far had worked, then this madness would be over. The government could set up an evacuation plan. The quarantine could be lifted and recovery could begin. He might even be able to go home, see his family, and work in their garden.

Ward was grateful his family was in Nova Scotia. That was about as far from this nightmare as a person could get and still be in Canada.

He was also grateful for functioning internet and electricity. He didn't believe in God, Buddha, or Allah, or anything really, but he was grateful they still had power and internet access. He had no clue how it was still working but he didn't want to think about what would happen if they lost it.

Things would get a lot darker really quickly. Metaphorically and literally.

So, a hydraulic press, guess he should order his men to start looking. And either way, it would lessen the power he had to share with Dr. Scordato and that certainly wasn't a bad thing in Ward's mind.

11

Through the bitterest colds it reached warmth. Land which evaded slumber and welcomed the virus, offering thousands of new lives to its own.

*   *   *

Treegar dropped her bag into the pile. They had found a decent haul that day. Stepping inside, and out of the bitter January winds, sent pin pricks of sweat across her body. Her ears, hands, and toes still ached from the relentless chill but her protective gear green-housed her natural body heat. Despite her overheating core, she wanted little more than to wrap her frigid fingers around something warm, preferably something that she could eat.

The main room was bustling as soldiers stripped off gear and rushed to the kitchen area for some food. Agatha sat at the table, greeting each soldier with a smile, laughing at their jokes, and looking so incredibly comfortable that it made Treegar uneasy.

She didn't have a good reason for her continued unease. Garner, Dr. Rudolph, Dr. Scordato, and literally everyone else said that she was fine. She wasn't infected, she didn't carry Xeno-1. But Treegar couldn't help it; something about Agatha made her uncomfortable.

She took a deep breath. She needed to get over this. Dr. Rudolph said it was PTSD, she said it was anxiety, she said that Treegar needed to develop coping strategies. She released her breath and took another.

In, hold, out.

She took a step forward.

Her hands clenched, digging her nails into her palms, the cut of them blunted by her gloves. In, hold, out. She took another step. Timing her breath to her movements helped, it gave her a focus. In, step, step, out, step, step. Repeat.

Reaching the end of the line meant that her steps no longer fell into rhythm. She held her breath a moment longer and counted in her head. In, one two three. Out, one two three. In, one two three. Out, one two three.

She was acutely aware of the distance between herself and Agatha. She was the only soldier still wearing their full gear, even that protection barely helped with the anxiety. The line moved forward. Treegar could smell the stew. The scent of cooked meat and vegetables perfuming the air, drawing in with her every breath. Her stomach clenched with hunger.

In, one two three.

Out, one two three.

Agatha laughed at something that one of the soldiers said. The breathy chuckle resonated through Treegar, vibrating her hypersensitive skin. She tried not to look.

In, one two three.

It was Garner. He had made her laugh.

Out, one two three.

Treegar could feel her agitation rising. Her hands trembled so she pulled them tight to her body, stiffening her muscles to force the tremors still.

In, one two three.

Out, one two three.

In, one two three.

Out, one two three.

She reached the front of the line. Lily handed her a bowl. Treegar focused on unclenching her hands and reaching out to accept the bowl. It sloshed in her trembling hands but the transfer of warmth was immediate.

In, one two three four.

She held the scent of the stew in for an extra moment, swiping a spoon from the table and rushing away. Her steps hurried and out of sync with her breathing.

Once at her cot, she placed her back to the wall and faced the room. Stew in one hand and spoon in the other she focused on her surroundings, cataloguing them and calming her heart. Agatha remained on the other side of the room. Garner was sitting with her. They were both staring at her with worried expressions. She forced herself to pull off her helmet and focus on putting the stew into her mouth. The stares and suppressed fear made her stomach clench. She took a bite, the flavours of the stew turned to ash in her mouth. She swallowed, it felt like lead crawling down her throat and landing heavily in her stomach. She did it again.

*　　*　　*

"You know what I think." Dr. Rudolph stated.

Treegar shrugged.

"I think that you are using the ongoing situation to justify pushing people away. You are emotionally distancing yourself to protect yourself from potential pain." She sighed and leaned toward Treegar.

"Look, I understand why you are doing this, the situation we are in," She gestured vaguely around, "is terrible. We could all die at any minute. It's smart to protect yourself. But don't you also think that if you could die at any moment that you might regret not taking the chance to actually live? I know it will be hard but you need to try and take steps forward. You can't stay still forever."

Treegar bit her lip. She knew that in many ways Dr. Rudolph was right, maybe even completely right. But opening up, being vulnerable at all, hadn't been her strong suit even before this situation started.

"I want you to try and take a step forward over the next few days, whatever that might look like to you." The doctor counseled.

"I'll do my best." Treegar agreed before standing and leaving the little office.

*   *   *

A step forward.

What did that even mean? Oh, she knew what Rudolph wanted it to mean. Forming human connections. Overcoming her fears. Blah, blah, blah. The doctor made it sound easy. There was nothing that sounded harder.

She worried the bottom of her lip between her teeth, gently picking away at the flaking top layer of skin until she tasted her own blood. It was metallic and familiar, almost a comfort. She sucked at that spot till the flavour and the blood were gone.

The main room buzzed with its usual between shifts activity. Half the room dozed in preparation for their own shifts while the other half engaged in leisure activities such as reading textbooks and manuals, card games, and in a few cases arts and crafts. At the other end of the room, Agatha puttered around the food station with Lily.

Garner was on the current shift. Treegar knew this because she had deliberately maneuvered herself on to an opposite shift from his. They had hardly spoken since he brought her to Dr. Rudolph. A combination of embarrassment and fear kept her away and encouraged her to keep him away too. She was too weak. That she had subjected him to even a portion of her exam, shamed her. That she wouldn't have been able to enter that room without him only made it worse. So, she had distanced herself from him, just like Dr. Rudolph said she was doing.

A step forward. Fine.

Fear felt easier to face than Garner.

She got up from her bed and began walking across the room. In, step, step, out, step, step. In and out, in and out.

The rhythm allowed her to cross the room quickly. It also stopped her from thinking about what she was doing.

Before she was ready, before she had been able to spare a thought for what this step would be, she had arrived. Barely two metres from Agatha, the old woman glanced up at her with a start.

"Hi." It came out forced and awkward, catching in her dry throat.

"Oh! Hi!" Agatha's greeting was equally forced but more cheerful.

There was a long, deeply uncomfortable pause. Treegar shifted her weight from one foot to the other, her mind blank.

"Would you like something?" Agatha finally asked, breaking the stalemate.

"Food." The word dropped like a fumbled football.

"Have a seat." Agatha waved at the small table that was used for everything from food prep to eating and cleaning up. It was clear now except for a small cutting board.

Treegar eased herself into a seat that allowed her to continue facing Agatha and watched as the woman retrieved a bowl from a stack and filled it from the ever-present food pot. This was weird. Her body was screaming that she wasn't safe. She should just get up and leave. Never mind the food, or the step, or whatever.

In, one two three. Out, one two three. She was in control of this.

"I'm glad you are settling in." Agatha chattered to fill the silence. "Vincent has been worried about you."

In, one two three. Out, one two three.

She focused on the movement of air through her lungs and not on the rising panic.

In, one two three.

"Here you are." Agatha held the bowl and spoon out to her. "You should talk to him. His shift should be back soon."

Treegar snatched them from Agatha and stood up abruptly. "Thanks." She muttered and sped across the room and back to her bunk.

Only when she reached the safety of her bunk did she realize that her hands had brushed Agatha's when she took the bowl and spoon. Her hands shook as she set the porridge down. She stared at the unbroken skin. They were fine. They looked like they always did. No acid burns.

In, one two three. Out, one two three.

She was safe. She was alive. She wasn't infected.

*   *   *

Agatha watched the retreating back of Corporal Treegar. The woman's presence no longer made her uncomfortable, instead over the past few weeks as she watched the younger woman turtle into herself, Agatha had grown to pity her.

Treegar had withdrawn to a point where Dr. Rudolph was worried. She hadn't confided in Agatha, doctor-patient confidentiality and all that, but Agatha could tell. Amber didn't exactly have the best poker face.

Agatha sighed. It was none of her business. Besides, she had precious little time or energy to invest it in someone else's business. Maybe she was being defeatist. Maybe she just needed to believe she would get better.

She snorted. Yeah, because the power of belief was what she'd been missing all along. Maybe that worked for some people but she could feel her body giving up. She felt so infinitely tired.

She had grown accustomed to the pain of her body, the subtle little ways it had already failed her. All she could do now was wait for the further failure as one system cascaded into the next.

The porridge would keep warm until the next shift woke. Agatha shuffled to her cot and eased her aching bones down onto its surface. Increasingly her body felt like a shell, a skeletal prison that trapped her mind in the pain of existence.

She closed her eyes and willed sleep to grant her temporary release.

*   *   *

Jason pulled a chair over to Agatha's bed and watched her sleep. The lines around her eyes softened and her mouth gaped slightly ajar. Her breath came heavy but stopped just short of a snore. He took comfort in her loud breathing.

Cancer hadn't been kind to her. Spots marked her sallow, papery skin. Lines etched into her face carved a portrait of pain, deepening with every day. She'd lost weight since he'd met her, her cheeks now held a hollow quality that emphasized the lines of her skull.

The rhythm of her breathing shifted, hitching for a moment before releasing once again. The creases around her eyes deepened as she pressed her lids tighter. Jason realized that he had been leaning towards her and quickly drew back. His timing proved good when Agatha fluttered her eyes open, squinting to filter out the soft partial light of the room.

"Hey." Jason greeted softly, his voice barely a whisper.

"Mmm, morning." She replied groggily. Agatha began to stretch but stopped suddenly retracting into herself with a flinch and a hiss.

"Are you doing okay?'

She puffed a laugh, "Well, I'm still here, aren't I?"

"So, terrible. As per usual." Jason quipped, only half joking.

Agatha turned a soft smile up at him, her forced levity failing completely to mask her pain. She began to try and sit up.

"Here." Jason offered, shifting out of his chair to gently grasp her arms and shoulders, his hands fluttering around her body to add additional support while the older woman pressed her way out of the mattress. Her bones pushed into the flesh of his palms, spine, elbow, shoulder, each making an impression barely softened by their thin cover of skin and fabric.

Once she was sitting up, he retreated back to his chair.

"How's it going?" Agatha asked, pulling the blanket so that it covered her legs and wrapped around her waist.

Jason noted that her eyes were still clouded and unfocused, whether it was from sleep or pain he couldn't be certain but it worried him nonetheless. "We have a plan to finish destroying the meteorite." He answered.

Her face lit up, smile lines smoothing out those left by pain. "That's wonderful! Do you and Jaspreet really think it will work?"

Jason had to glance away, "Maybe. We hope it will. Honestly, we have all but abandoned normal scientific practices at this point. Now we are just working on hopes and theories. If this works, great. If it doesn't… well the virus has spread to other, better equipped, facilities. We aren't the only ones working on a cure."

Agatha leaned to her left to catch Jason's eyes again, "So, you're saying that one way or another this is it, at least as far as we can go here?"

Jason nodded, "Either way, there won't be any reason to maintain this facility after this."

Agatha looked off into the middle distance. Jason noted with a pang that her eyes had cleared up significantly during their short conversation. "Well, then I have a request."

Jason leaned forward, bracing his weight to rest on his knees. "Anything. What is it?"

She sighed and seemed to shrink into herself, "We both know I don't have much longer," Jason opened his mouth to deny this but Agatha spoke over his protests, blatantly ignoring him as she did so, "When you leave this place, I'd like you to bring my rings to my daughters. I know now that I should have left them with them before I came up here looking for Maria. But it's too late now and I can't go back. I understand that you may want to head east, but could you go south first? Please?"

Jason snapped his gaping mouth closed. He had no idea what to say. Almost on instinct he found himself nodding, agreeing, through tear-stung eyes and blurred vision.

Agatha huffed out another breathy, pain laden, laugh, "Don't be like that. It's a miracle I've lived this long! Oh, oh come here!" She reached out and grasped his shirt sleeve and tugged. Jason couldn't resist and rolled out of his chair and on to his knees beside the bed. The two wrapped arms around each other in comfort and friendship. Jason carefully kept his grip gentle, while Agatha squeezed him tight to her bones.

12

One benefit of the cold was in the longevity of the bodies. The ones of the warm land had no such benefit. They submitted to decay more quickly than those wrapped in chill. This forced the virus to spread quicker, seeing now the wisdom in their youthful race. Different methods befitted different times.

*   *   *

Charissa double checked Timothy's outfit while he double checked hers. Penelope stood at the top of the entryway and wrung her hands. Both Sophia and Atticus were still in bed, which was for the best since neither had taken the news that their daddy was going to go outside very well.

Once they had finished their check both Timothy and Charissa looked back at Penelope and forced smiles. Timothy gave a little salute and then awkwardly opened his arms. Penelope stumbled down the stairs in her haste to throw herself at him.

"You come back to me; you hear?" She mumbled into his chest.

Charissa glanced away and adjusted the strap of the plastic Frozen backpack she had borrowed for the supply run. Penelope had convinced them to wait another week after their initial agreement before starting their runs. Unlike the previous silence, that week had been filled with planning and preparation. Nearly every last piece of plastic clothing in the house had been fitted into outfits for Charissa and Timothy. Rain boots and coats weren't enough, she wouldn't let them go out without 100% of their bodies protected in some way. Charissa was decked out in a welding mask, plastic rain jacket and hood, plastic sun hat, rubber fishing overalls, and yellow dishwashing gloves. The outfit did not breathe, but it did protect her entire body with at least one layer, if not two layers, of plastic. Timothy was wearing a similarly fashionable ensemble.

When Penelope and Timothy separated, Penelope turned and gave her sister a much shorter hug. When she pulled away, she gave Charissa a look that said, *bring him back*. Charissa nodded, she hoped she brought both of them back safe and sound.

They unlocked the door and Timothy stepped out first, hunting rifle lifted and ready in case of any movement. He used his boot to push away the rotting remains of whatever infected creature or creatures had been scraping at their door. The chill morning air slipped through the plastic outfit, exploiting its every weakness. Charissa lifted her rifle and slipped outside behind Timothy with Penelope quickly shutting and locking the door behind them.

Deep frost gripped the world and immobilized the infected creatures, Timothy and Charissa picked their way through the maze their bodies created. Her skin prickled with hyperawareness. With great care they made their way to the next-door neighbor's house. Timothy gently tried the front door but it was unsurprisingly locked. He then led the way around to the back of the house.

The gate resisted opening. Timothy gave it a quick, sharp shove with his shoulder and the frozen hinges swung open. Charissa watched behind them as Timothy did this, her eyes catching on the mutated forms melting into the ground. In the early morning light, she made out dark and matted fur, feathers, and bloated distended bellies on nearly skeletal forms. Eyes stared at her from frozen weeping faces, more than one creature sported a bloody or pus-filled hole where an eye used to be. In all cases the creatures looked diseased, neglected and starved.

Charissa shuddered and glanced behind her at Timothy before

moving to follow him through the gate.

They slid along the path to the back of the house. Timothy moved slowly, tension radiating from his stiff back. Charissa tried to relax her shoulders as sharp pin pricks of pain bit into her shoulder blades. She pulled in a shallow breath, releasing it slowly to prevent the warm wet air from her lungs from fogging up the welding mask.

The yard had fewer creatures than Timothy and Penelope's yard. There was a large hole in the fence separating the two yards. Charissa kept moving her gaze from behind them back to that hole, half expecting some horrific creature to drag itself through it and attack them.

Timothy edged past the hole and turned to sidestep up the three stairs to the deck. The back door was locked but this time Timothy quickly rammed his shoulder against the door. The door creaked but didn't give. He stepped back and hit it again to no effect.

Charissa watched the yard nervously. Sweat trickled down the back of her neck. The unfamiliar weight of the hunting rifle sat awkwardly in her arms, her muscles quickly growing tired and beginning to burn from the exertion.

Timothy leaned back and kicked the door. The wood splintered around the frame and a swift follow up kick sent the door swinging inward. He surveyed the interior, allowing his eyes a moment to adjust before moving inside.

Charissa followed, while the early morning sun barely illuminated the yard, the interior of the house was still wreathed in shadow and it took her eyes a moment to adjust. Once inside she eased the broken door closed behind her and followed Timothy deeper into the house.

A fine layer of dust coated all of the surfaces. Combined with the dim early morning light, it accentuated the grey scale and plunged the house into a dull sort of surrealism. It felt dead, soulless and forgotten.

Timothy led them straight to the kitchen with a confidence that brought uncomfortable questions to Charissa's mind. How many times has he been in this house? How well had he known the owners? She didn't voice these thoughts, they had more important things to focus on.

"Take what you can carry, I'll stand watch." Timothy directed.

Charissa sighed in relief and gave her arms a much-needed rest by lowering her rifle and leaning it against the bottom cupboards. She began opening cupboards and assessing their contents. The first two cupboards held only dishes, then there was a spice and tea cupboard which she quickly emptied into her Frozen backpack. The fourth cupboard was filled with dry goods, including pasta noodles, ramen, and instant potatoes. She fit about half of them into her bag before she could barely zip it closed. She passed it to Timothy and took his Dinosaur backpack and put the rest of the cupboard's contents into it.

The lower cupboards were more fruitful and made Charissa wish she had thought to start there. Canned goods, four, sugar, and rice. There was so much that she knew they had no chance of bringing it all back with them today. The flour and rice alone would necessitate their own trips since they could only carry what would fit in the backpacks.

"We'll have to come back. There's too much for us to carry this time." She said while swinging the now full dinosaur backpack on and lifting her rifle again.

"Let's go." Timothy hitched his gun a little higher on his shoulder and set back out through the back door.

Charissa resisted the urge to sigh in relief, they were heading back, it was almost over.

The world had grown brighter during their brief sojourn in the house. No morning birds sang and the only sound was a slight scraping coming from the hole in the fence. Charissa's whole focus narrowed in on the opening as a black lump began oozing its way through.

Timothy continued down the stairs and retraced his steps completely unawares of the creature inching its way toward him.

"What is that?" Charissa gasped, her mind grappling with the shape of the infected. Something about it was familiar but how she wasn't immediately certain.

Timothy reacted to her question and stiffened, stopping in his tracks and scanning the yard. His gaze caught on the creature, "Luna?"

"Come on, we gotta move!" Charissa urged. As what may have once been Luna got its bulk through the gap it began to pick up speed, no longer easing along at a glacial rate but instead leaving a discernible trail behind it.

Timothy wrenched his gaze from the creature and rushed around the corner of the house. Charissa raced down the stairs and followed him through the gate and to the front of the house. Both moving with far less caution than they had on their initial journey. In mere moments they stood in front of their front door.

Charissa's heart pounded and she shifted from foot to foot, watching behind them while Timothy knocked out the signal.

Knock,

Knock, knock, knock,

Knock,

Pause, knock, knock.

Almost before he made the final knock Penelope had the door

unlocked and was ushering them inside.

"Take your boots off first. Here, wipe them off. Don't get any of that stuff on you." She insisted while handing them each a ragged towel and then stepping back to watch them anxiously.

"Did you know that thing?" Charissa asked while doing as Penelope told her.

Timothy shuddered, "I think that was Luna, the Johnson's dog." He sighed and wrenched the rainboots off. With a nearly silent curse he collapsed on the bottom stair. "I hoped to never see that." He was silent for a minute.

Charissa finished wiping off her boots and removing them then placed the soiled rag into a plastic bag. She tucked her boots out of the way and began removing and hanging up the rest of her outfit.

Timothy shook his head and stood to continue removing his outfit. "I knew it had happened. I mean, how could it not? I just… I just hoped I'd never see it, have it confirmed. You know?"

Charissa had no idea what to say to that so the two of them just continued removing their gear in silence and if she saw Penelope and Timothy holding each other and crying later, well she just distracted the kids and let them have their moment of grief.

13

It settled into a rhythm, different parts of it playing in concert with the others. The center held the constant beat while the outer edges grew and trilled. It could feel footsteps as the beat of drums, attacks as the mating calls of birds, and searching as the unerring melody. It found beauty within its own harmony.

*　　*　　*

The lights flickered again.

Jason swore and slammed the lid of his laptop closed. Power was becoming increasingly unreliable, not that they were running any tests currently, but it threatened to cut off even their tenuous connection to the outside world.

This couldn't continue. Three days ago, the water had stopped, leaving them reliant on melted snow for hydration and with the infected frozen in so much of their surroundings each drop felt like a dangerous game of chance. Food supplies were constantly diminishing and now the power was going.

The only comfort was that while it might flicker it had always come back on. So far. The depth of winter seemed to be passing, bringing on the storms of early spring. Sudden thaws followed dismally by a sharp return to sub-zero temperatures.

The lights flickered out again. He counted the darkness, one two three four five six seven eight. The lights came on.

*　　*　　*

"Jason! Jason, wake up! They've found it! They've found one!" Jaspreet's excited voice broke through his dreams, pushing back the reaching rotting limbs and yanking him back into reality.

"Wha…?" Jason managed while sitting up. They pooled in his lap, exposing his shoulders to a cold draft. He wanted to pull the material back up, to use them to hide from the cruelty he found both in his dreams and real life.

"The hydraulic press!" Jaspreet exclaimed; she really was too excited for how blurry Jason's mind felt.

He dumbly watched her pace in front of him for at least four steps before her words sunk in. He practically leapt from the cot.

"Where is it? Can you leave now?" The questions flew out his mouth even as he stumbled to find his footing.

Jaspreet nodded, loose bits of her straight black hair flying about her head. "That's why I grabbed you. As soon as we're ready we are heading out. Can't get this over soon enough!" With that she twirled on her heel and walked away, a distinct swagger in her step.

Jason couldn't help the smile that spread across his face. He grabbed an extra sweater and pulled it over his rumpled clothing while following closely behind Dr. Nagi.

"Is it prepped?" He asked once he caught up.

"My assistants are doing the final touches as we speak."

"Excellent."

Jaspreet slipped on a military issue protective jacket and Jason noticed that she was already wearing the standard pants. She looked different in military garb, he wasn't sure exactly how, just different. It struck him abruptly that in all their planning they hadn't really talked about what it would be like for one of them to leave this place and go outside. As much as he longed for some fresh air, he did not envy her the dangers that lurked outdoors.

By the time she was sufficiently protected, Ward and several other soldiers had joined them.

"It's a three-hour trek, Johnson and Anker will be your guides." Ward waved to the two soldiers to step forward. "The rest of this group will accompany you there but their primary objective will be obtaining food. If you encounter any trouble, you have to get down and let the professionals handle it, do you understand me?"

Jaspreet nodded.

One of Jaspreet's assistants rushed up the hallway with a duffle bag clutched under their arms. They passed it carefully to Jaspreet who nodded and murmured a quick thanks.

"Let's get to it."

Jason tried to project the calm assurance that Jaspreet seemed to carry so effortlessly but found it hard to still the agitation fluttering in his belly. What if this worked? What if it didn't?

* * *

The cruel February wind swept across the snow-covered landscape tearing at the drifts of snow as easily as it tore the memory of warmth from Jaspreet, picking up tiny shards of frozen snow and throwing it back up into the air at her. In an instant it slipped through the weaknesses in her layers and exploited them for its own gain. She shivered in a futile attempt at rebuilding her lost heat.

Jaspreet forced her legs forward, following the line of soldiers making their way along a well-worn path cut through the snow.

The path snaked past patches of discolouration keeping her distracted by the sheer number of infected who had converged on their location. When the path straightened out, she hazarded a glance back the way they had come. The hospital was nothing but a distant, desaturated haze on the horizon.

* * *

Jason waited impatiently in the lab, checking and rechecking the samples. He ran every baseline test he could think of double and triple checking the results against their records. He had no idea how long it would take Jaspreet and the soldiers to reach the hydraulic press so after every test they were capable of performing had been done and he'd cleaned and organized until there was truly nothing left to do, he finally left the lab.

He'd skipped breakfast, rushing to the lab the moment Jaspreet had left but the warm aroma of hot food made him regret that decision. He wove his way through the cots and strewn bags and ladled himself a bowl of whatever concoction was in the general pot and took it to the nearby table where Lil was slicing root vegetables.

"Morning." She greeted him with a toothy grin. "You're here late. What kept you?"

"Running baseline tests. Nothing special," he dug into his food, ignoring her sharp gaze. He didn't want to get her hopes up but keeping his anticipation from affecting his voice and movements was impossible.

"You're not acting like it's nothing special."

"Yeah, well." Jason shrugged and looked around. His eyes fell on Agatha's cot. "Agatha laying down again?"

"No,"

He glanced back at Lil, noticing how her brow had furrowed and her habitual smile was completely gone.

"She hasn't gotten up yet."

"What?" Jason gasped, that wasn't like Agatha. Even in her pain she was a go-getter, often getting up ridiculously early to ensure that food was fresh and ready for the first shift of the day. He paused and considered the time, it was at least three hours into the morning shift. That meant she had overslept by a good four hours. His heart sank, something was very wrong.

He left his bowl on the table and went to Agatha's bedside. In the cool fluorescent her skin looked pale as snow. Her breathing was so soft as to be barely perceptible. Some movement during her slumber had knocked her blanket down to her waist. Jason grabbed the edge and pulled it up to her chin, gently tucking it in so that she wouldn't lose too much body heat. As he did so his own warm hands brushed against her cool cheek.

"Mmm?" She hummed, her eyes fluttering open but still unseeing.

"Sorry, I didn't mean to wake you," Jason apologised.

"'s okay," She muttered, smacking her lips together and blinking slowly. She turned her head to face him but instead of recognition her brow furrowed in confusion, her clouded eyes searching his face without recognition.

"How are you doing? You want some breakfast?" He asked, desperate to make her recognize him but unwilling to acknowledge her confusion by outrightly reminding her of who he was.

"Breakfast?" her eyes cleared a little, "What time is it?"

"It's a little past 10am. You must be hungry."

She blinked a few more times, awareness and recognition slowly clearing the lines on her face. "I can't believe I slept so late. Help me up, I'll get breakfast going." She reached out with a twig like arm and waved for him to help pull her up.

Jason reached forward and grasped her arm, pulling her forward even as she exercised surprising strength in gripping him and pulling herself forward. Together they got her sitting up and then Jason helped her swing her legs over the edge of the cot. She scooted her bum to the edge of the bed. He hovered over her as she pushed herself up and forward, off the bed and toward the kitchen. Her knees wobbled and Jason gently grabbed her shoulders to steady her.

Like that they walked the short distance to the kitchen where he directed her into the chair he had so recently vacated, his own bowl sitting and cooling in front of her.

"Oh? What's this?" She looked up across the table at Lil, whose own face was creased with concern. She then picked up Jason's spoon and took a small bite of the stew he had abandoned.

Jason was far less concerned that she was finishing his breakfast than that she still seemed unsure of who either he or Lil were and where she was. He moved around so she could see him again.

She looked up between bites and gave him a soft smile. The tension in his chest eased a little at that look. "This is good." She puffed, "Thank you."

Jason could feel his heart breaking and had to turn away, he could no longer face his friend when she no longer seemed to remember that that was what she was to him.

*　　*　　*

The workshop had been ravaged by the winter and neglect. Jaspreet was pretty sure she was going to need a tetanus booster after being inside. She watched the soldier ahead of her carefully, matching the placement of her feet to theirs. They worked their way around fallen and rusted equipment, broken glass, and drifting snow, the weight of the duffle bag resting heavily on her back and nearly throwing her balance off a few times.

Jaspreet had been shifting the bag back and forth through the journey redistributing its weight as evenly as she could around her body. After months confined in the hospital and on restricted diets, she wasn't at her prime physical fitness. This meant alternating between burning and aching, sharp pricks of white-hot pain lancing through her shoulders alternating with the jelly inducing ache in her knees. Unfortunately the famed endorphin rush from exercise had yet to kick in.

Daylight dappled through holes in the roof, lighting up the drifting snow till it nearly glowed in the relative gloom. Standing and fallen machines cast strange shadows, shifting around them into a nearly living mass. Things flickered at the edge of her vision but disappeared the moment she turned her head.

The lead soldier, Anker, stopped at one of the machines. It featured a wide metal plunger over a solid, inset base. "This is it." He announced, "Johnson, go see if you can rig up the power." Jaspreet glanced back to catch the end of Johnson's sharp nod and watch the man turn and step away. "Doctor, let's get that thing set up. I can't guarantee how much juice Johnson will be able to get us, we gotta be ready."

She swung the bag to her front and placed it as gently as her tired arms could manage on the ground. Once it was on the ground, she unzipped the main pocket and withdrew the remaining portion of the meteorite. The metal lattice was wrapped tightly in layers of protective material, including a lead lined apron taken from the hospital's X-ray department. She was too exhausted for real joy when the thing was discarded but she certainly wasn't sorry to see it gone.

Jaspreet was too tired for real emotions and mechanically unwrapped the other protective layers. The strange alloy was a pale silver, with a hint of blue opalescence. Even in the dim light it shimmered in a beautiful, alien way. The strands looked like nothing more than spun sugar, fragments no thicker than a piece of cooked pasta wove through and around one another into an intricate and mesmerising pattern. It looked like lace, too delicate for the strength and durability it had shown in her lab and only the size of a grapefruit.

She moved to place the lattice on the pad beneath the hydraulic press's plunger. In that moment she gave in to her instincts and attempted to crush the thing between her own hands. Her weakened arms shook for only a moment as the unrelenting structure of the meteorite pressed into her gloved palms before she gave up and dropped the thing into its place.

Jaspreet and Anker moved away, shielding themselves as best they could behind other equipment, most of which were unfamiliar to her and thus strange and mysterious even before the obfuscation of time and neglect were added. She leaned heavily on the structure, allowing the minutes to sweep past her weary mind. It felt like a moment and like forever before Johnson's voice broke the silence.

"I think I've got it."

Jaspreet lurched back to alertness, her eyes returning from staring into the middle distance to focus on the shimmering remains of the meteorite. Unconsciously she edged closer, needing to see this ended in a visceral part of her soul.

"Here we go. Let's hope this works." Anker flipped the on switch for the hydraulic press and the thing roared to life, filling the warehouse with thrumming white noise.

The press began its descent, the plunger quickly meeting with the top of the lattice structure. There was a pregnant pause while the machine whirred and chugged, the metal of the press seeming to give way both above and below the structure. The lattice bit into the plunger before bulging for a fraction of a moment and then shattering outward.

Jaspreet's mind didn't register the break before pain exploded from her thigh. She gasped in shock while dropping to the floor. Her hands reflexively grabbed the injured appendage, hovering over the jutting out shard as every movement sent a scraping, stabbing lance of pain through the muscles and bone. It was only that pain which kept her from tearing the offending object from her thigh. The pulse of blood and pain overwhelmed the decreasing whir of the hydraulic press as it powered down.

Jaspreet put a hand on her leg, spreading her fingers around the offending shrapnel and putting pressure around the wound. She fumbled through the pile of discarded wrappings, pulling out the softest thing her gloves touched. The fabric had once been a hospital sheet but had recently served as one of the layers covering the lattice on its journey here.

Anker stood back from her and shook his head when she looked up at him for help. She knew from the look on his face that she was on her own. Something about this situation, whether it was the nature of her injury or something else, meant that she would have to deal with this herself.

Releasing her hold on her injury, she grasped the fabric with both hands and pulled. Adrenaline lent strength to her weary arms and the fabric gave, ripping in a straight line. She pulled again and again until the sheet was in two strips. Then she folded one of the strips and wrapped a portion of it above the shrapnel. She pulled it tight and then, gritting her teeth and hoping that she was doing the right thing, she yanked the chunk out of her leg.

She gasped and hissed. Her leg felt like it was on fire for a moment and then the pain receded into an aching throb. As quickly as she could she wrapped the remainder of the strip's length around her injury and tied it off. It wasn't pretty but it should keep her blood where it belonged, inside of her.

"Can you walk?" Anker demanded of her.

Jaspreet waved her gloves in the air, "I don't know. I guess I'll have to. Can you help me up?" She held her right hand out to him, noticing as she did that parts of her fingers glistened with her own blood. The realization made her stomach churn.

Anker shook his head, "Can you get up on your own?" Something about his stance, the way his grip had shifted on his gun, made Jaspreet certain that if she couldn't get up and get herself back to base by her own power, then he had orders to shoot her out here.

It was a terrifying realization and served to power her from the floor back into a standing position. She leaned heavily on her other leg, pulling on the nearby equipment to lighten her load, but she got there and she got there fast. "I'll be fine." She assured, desperate to make him stop looking at her like he was one second from ending her life.

She eased her weight onto her injured leg, each movement sent a quiver of pain through her injury. Her leg could hold her weight, she tested it further by making the short walk to the hydraulic press.

"We should pack up the pieces. we might need them for further testing." She still held the chunk that had hit her and using her other hand she pried out a few bits that were stuck into the metal of the hydraulic press. She looked back at Anker, whose grip on his gun had relaxed slightly, "Come on, I'm going to need your help, heaven only knows how far the pieces were flung."

He bent down and picked up a piece that had landed near his feet and began helping her. Jaspreet released a held breath and relaxed a little, at least he no longer seemed like her imminent executioner.

Johnson rejoined them from wherever he had been controlling the hydraulic presses power flow and saw what they were apparently doing. He joined in on the search with no prompting and no questions about why Jaspreet now had an improvised bandage around her leg.

It only took them about fifteen minutes to find the largest pieces and about five more minutes after that before Anker announced that that was good enough. Jaspreet thought about arguing but was honestly too wiped from all the unusual exercise, her injury, and the exhaustion of coming down from an adrenaline high.

She just shrugged, zipped up the much lighter duffle bag that now only contained the lattice fragments and swung it onto her back.

"Dr. Nagi, if you could take point." Anker ordered. "I'm sure you can follow our trail back."

Jaspreet nodded but tried not to allow thoughts of bullets in her back distract her from the painful act of placing one foot in front of the other. It occurred to her that Anker might be concerned about her turning, that the lattice fragment might have infected her. If that was the case, and if she did turn, then maybe a bullet in her back was the best option.

14

Garner was cleaning his gear. His arms rippled as he changed his grip, seeking any trace of dirt or grime. The thin sinew and muscle bore testament to the sparse, hard living he had dealt with over the past several months.

Treegar tried to remember if she had ever noticed his arms before, before winter and war stripped them of any softness that they may have originally held. There was a vague memory of them wrapped around her, their warmth pulling the cracked and broken parts of her back together. But that memory was over laid by the harder, more familiar, more recent memory of him protecting her from a nightmare.

The echo of his touch made her heart pound. She turned away and tried to think of something else. It was too quiet here. In this building where they were 'safe'. Her thoughts had too much space. She was better out there, where her senses kept her troubled thoughts at bay, where her anxiety was a survival tactic and not a liability.

Her body felt as restless as her mind. She wasn't good at sitting and waiting, nothing to do. It was harder than fighting the infected. Her skin tingled with memories. She pushed down the hairs on her arms through her long sleeves. Dr. Rudolph wanted her to get used to life without the gear again but it left her feeling exposed.

In, one two three. Out, one two three.

Maybe she should force herself to talk to Garner. At least thinking about him kept the panic down.

With a frustrated scoff at her own weakness, Treegar pushed up from her bed. She felt Garner look at her. For a moment she hesitated, she had his attention, she should go over and say something. Instead, she turned away, his gaze digging holes in her back.

She pushed herself to walk over to the kitchen area. Agatha was leaning against the table. Treegar counted her steps and breaths, closing the distance. Her rational mind reminded her that Agatha wouldn't and couldn't harm her, but she focused on the calming techniques anyways.

Agatha swayed and braced herself with both hands. Treegar lost count of her breaths.

Agatha hit the floor with a gasp. Treegar was beside her in an instant, grabbing the woman and shaking her gently. Her hands fluttered over the older woman's skeletal frame.

"Agatha?" She cried in shock.

Agatha's eyes rolled back and she didn't respond.

Treegar glanced up for assistance. Garner was halfway across the room, concern wrinkling his brow.

Carefully, she eased herself and Agatha up. The old woman draped over her arms like a rag doll. Treegar tried to smooth her gait as she carried Agatha to the nearest bed and eased her into it. The woman weighed hardly anything, it felt impossible that a human could survive and have so little mass.

Treegar felt her mind catching on that one fact, circling it and questioning, while she slid her arms out from under the unconscious woman's body.

"What happened?" Garner questioned.

Treegar sighed and looked at him. His eyes were darting between Agatha's face and her own. "I don't know, she just collapsed. We need a doctor."

"Right, yes. I'll bring one back." Garner spun and took a few steps before pausing and surveying the room.

Treegar looked away from him, back to Agatha's face. The woman looked old. Not in the pinched way that truly old people look, with their eyes and mouth pulled in toward their nose, but in the way that sick people look old. Like she was more skeleton than person. Her cheeks sunken, her skin a papery yellow. Treegar reached out and adjusted her hands. They were cold, the blue veins jutting out from translucent skin pulled loosely over tendons and bone.

She didn't know why but she slowly lowered into a squat, holding on to Agatha's cold hand. She focused on the shuddering rise and fall of Agatha's chest. Up and down. Up and down. Her own breathing unconsciously matching it.

A shuddering inhale. A slow release. Longer than Treegar's lungs were comfortable with. Before the next inhale, they were burning for oxygen.

"What happened?" Dr. Rudolph came rushing up with Garner trailing behind.

"She collapsed." Even to her ears her voice sounded flat, dead, void of natural human emotion. She looked down at the cool, dry, skin covered bones in her hands, they were barely alive, barely human and yet seemed so familiar. An unfamiliar sense of kinship rose within her.

Treegar watched Dr. Rudolph snap on a pair of gloves and then reach down to check Agatha's neck for a pulse. Treegar could feel the reedy beat through Agatha's wrist, she was alive, for now. At least as alive as Treegar felt.

A warm hand touched her shoulder. "Are you okay, Madison?" Garner asked. Treegar wanted to crawl inside the warmth of his voice. Unconsciously, she leaned into his hand, her back bumping into his legs.

Her shoulders started to tremble, a soul deep chill fighting against the warmth that Garner freely offered her. He slid down and wrapped his arms around her. Agatha's hand slipped out of Madison's grip and fell, hanging limp from the bed.

Dr. Rudolph circled Agatha, poking and timing things against their wrist watch. Madison and Garner sat back, on the cold floor, and grasped each other. It wasn't until they bustled away that Madison realized that Garner had done it again, he had sensed her falling apart and had held her together.

She was too stunned to move. His arms still wrapped around her body, sheltering her from the room, from the world. The trembling slowed. Her breath evened out and began to match his.

"You, okay?" he whispered into her ear, his breath tickling her and sending loose bits of hair fluttering against her skin.

"Yeah." She sighed.

He pulled away, leaving a vacuum of cold where he had been. Madison felt the warmth leak from her body. She shuddered and rubbed her hands up and down over her arms to generate more warmth.

Garner stood and reached down, offering his hand to Madison. She released her arms and took his hand. She tried to prevent her body from leaning into his as he pulled her up. It was a struggle but once she was standing, he released her hand and turned away.

Madison swallowed and refocused on Agatha. The woman hadn't shifted in the long minutes since Madison had let go of her hand. With a careful exhale she reached out and gently recaptured Agatha's hand and moved it onto the bed.

"Here, have a seat." Garner offered, sliding a chair behind Madison. When she glanced back at him, he had already turned to grab a second chair.

Madison looked at the chair, then Garner, and then at Agatha. She rubbed her lips together. Agatha's hand was so cold. She stepped away from the chair and the bed. The next cot was made up with military precision. It took a few sharp tugs to release the tightly folded corners and then the blanket was in her hands. She shook it out and threw it over Agatha. As it settled down the lab tech grabbed the other side and helped tuck it in.

Madison noticed that her breath was coming in short shallow pants, her skin felt tight and her hands were clammy. Her eyes darted to the other end of the room, to the shadows near her own bed. She took a step. She thought of her breathing and tried to elongate each breath, pulling air deeper into her lungs.

"Madison?" Garner's voice broke through the rising panic. "Where are you going?"

Words were too difficult. Madison took another step. Her skin prickled and pulled; every follicle raised in warning.

"Hey," Garner's impossibly warm hands wrapped gently around her arms, pushing the raised hairs down uncomfortably. "Come on, we shouldn't leave her alone." He murmured.

Madison resisted for a moment before her body caved back into his warmth. Even as her skin soaked up his radiant heat, a core of cold remained deep within her. She glanced back at Agatha, struck again by the feeling of kinship between herself and the near-corpse of a woman. Her rising panic temporarily abated but lurking at the edges of her mind, threatening and looming. She allowed Garner to direct her body back to the waiting pair of chairs.

15

Jason watched as the samples in his lab shifted. One by one he prepared them for testing, already knowing that if their desperate act of breakinging the lattice hadn't exactly killed Xeno-1 that it had done something.

It didn't take long for the first tests to come back. Xeno-1 was acting erratically, the individual cells shifting and changing in ways they never had previously. it wasn't mutating but it did appear in a state of sudden flux. Were they the death-throes of a super virus or something else entirely?

The electromagnetic field between samples was remarkably diminished, while there were still electromagnetic fields around each individual sample, they no longer seemed to be in a state of entanglement as they had previously seemed. This could be crucial in the search for a cure. If they did find a cure then the individual infected beings wouldn't be able to create an immunity before they had a chance to inoculate them. It also meant that if a vaccine were created it might be able to remain truly effective even if inoculated people had more than one encounter with Xeno-1.

The next several hours revealed little more in quantitative data but in qualitative there were a multitude of changes in the samples. One of his longest held samples even died out during the course of the testing. It was incredible and Jason couldn't help but feel a sense of elation.

*　　　*　　　*

Jaspreet stamped snow off of her boots, the action reverberating up her leg and aggravating her thigh. Anker and Johnson kept watch on her through the whole trip back. Jaspreet hated the way their hands were always hovering near their guns. It made her neck itch and her stomach knot.

Entering the building was a relief. The immediate absence of wind and glaring sunlight was like walking into a warm cave. While the darkness left her blinking and straining her eyes, the relative warmth and firm floor nearly made her collapse. It was so nice to be back. To be safe again.

She trudged through the labyrinth of corridors, the lights overhead only flickering once. Jaspreet worked her way to Jason's lab, she needed to check three things: had their plan worked, the fragments, and her leg. In that exact order. Nothing, not even her health, was more important than the success of their mission.

Anker and Johnson trailed behind her, past the point where they should have peeled off to make their report to Ward. Jaspreet propelled herself forward partly on sheer stubbornness and partly on the promise of a chair inside the lab. The door loomed close in front of her.

Her knees ached and her legs trembled, but she pulled the door handle and barely kept himself from falling into the familiar room.

"Jaspreet!" Jason exclaimed, whether from surprise or shock, Jaspreet was too tired to discern.

She nodded at him, or at least she thought she did. The room swam in front of her and her body reacted sluggishly. She reached out to the counter to brace herself, just as her injured leg gave out. She hung for a moment, clutching between the handle of the open door and the countertop, barely keeping her body from pitching to the floor for the second time that day.

"Doctor!" Jason leapt forward and caught her shoulders. With his support, Jaspreet eased herself onto a stool and took the weight from her legs. They hung like strips of raw bacon, limp and half melted. Even her bones felt soft and loose in a numbly uncomfortable way. "What happened?"

"Oh? Nothing, just walking…" Jaspreet trailed off, her mind whirling like a broken starter, simply failing to engage. Jason began undoing the bandage on her leg. "Oh, that… a piece…" She sought the right words to describe what had happened. But she felt fuzzy, her thoughts circling but never completing. "Hit me. It's not deep."

"Step away from him, Doctor." Anker stated loud and clear, his voice booming through the silent laboratory.

"What?" Jason protested, "She's injured. She needs medical attention."

"Until we know for sure that she isn't infected, no one touches her."

"Infected? Don't be ridiculous, and even if she were, I am wearing gloves." He held up his reused but sanitized working gloves, as though the sight of them would change the steel like resolve in Ankers' declaration.

Jaspreet dropped the bag she had carried the whole way back and let it fall to the floor with a clinking thud. She swayed and leaned against the counter and she closed her eyes.

There was a pregnant pause until she fluttered her deep brown eyes back open and fixed them on Jason, Anker, and Johnson. She reached up and pulled off her helmet, her hair fighting to go in every direction possible, including right into her mouth. She blew the offending strands out and dropped her helmet beside the bag.

"We need to test the fragments. See if the readings have changed. If it worked." She gestured to the bag on the floor, her hand making a flapping motion despite her attempt at a more precise movement.

Jason nodded and stepped away to scoop the pack up, his eyes briefly flickering to the gun Anker held at the ready and back to Jaspreet's injured leg. He silently moved to a bench, put the bag down, and began pulling out its fragmented contents.

Jaspreet removed her gloves, discarding them to the floor, and began to fumble at the bandage herself. The knot slipped from her fingers over and over. She dug her nails into it and tried to force it to loosen simply by strength of will. It laughed at her feeble will. A hand rested over her own and stilled her fumbling. She looked up at the lightly salted black top of Jason's head as he bent over her leg and expedited the bandage removal by using scissors.

Anker stared at the pair of them with ill disguised disgust and worry but now that the damage was done said nothing more.

Jaspreet hissed as he eased the fabric away from her injury. The dried blood and fabric clinging to the skin and reopening the barely sealed wound.

"You need to remove your pants." Jason stated, it was more of an embarrassed sigh than a command but Jaspreet treated it as one nonetheless. She fumbled at her zipper, fingers slipping before finally grasping the tiny metal tab and directing it downward. She lost her grip about halfway and before she could regain it Jason once again took over. He unzipped the protective outer layer of pants and spread the plastic fabric wide, revealing the deeply bloodstained pants she wore underneath. The worn fabric was pressed into the wound and fresh dark blood burbled gently out of the newly reopened gash.

Steadying her breath took her a moment after seeing the extent of her injury. After a long moment she pulled in her stomach and began to work the top button loose on her pants. They clung tight to her skin, unrelenting in their hold on her. "We'll need to cut them," she finally admitted.

Dr. Scordato nodded and picked up the scissors he had used on the bandage from the counter. His hands were firm and efficient as he forced them through the thick denim.

Jaspreet bit back a hiss as the wound was pulled this way and that by Jason's removal of her pants. He gently worked the denim off of her skin and out of where it entered her wound. Dark sticky blood held the fabric in place, slowly drying to keep the denim adhered to her. Jason was efficient and unrelenting. Jaspreet had to dig her fingers into the solid countertop to keep her leg from twitching away from his ministrations.

When the fabric was finally clear and the wound revealed it proved almost a disappointment compared to the blood and pain. At the centre top of all the oozing blood was a puncture wound no larger than the tip of Jaspreet's pinky.

Dr. Scordato stood and brought over antiseptic and began cleaning the area. Jaspreet gritted her teeth against the sting of antiseptic fluid touching the wound. Her thigh was almost white once the red and black-brown blood was removed though the area around the puncture remained an irritated and raised red.

Jason probed the wound, "It looks clear. Does it feel like there is anything in there?"

Jaspreet shook her head. It felt raw and bruised but no splinters or fragments irritated it.

"Good. I'm going to wrap you back up. Hopefully we can prevent infection from setting in."

Jaspreet looked away from the wound and glanced around the lab. Anker had, at some point, been replaced by a different soldier but Johnson remained at the door.

"Okay, that should do it. We will need to keep an eye on it to make sure it heals right, and you should try to stay off it as much as you can." Jason said. "Now, I'm sure you want to know about the results of your efforts. While they aren't conclusive, I can verify that breaking the lattice did something."

"Really?" Jaspreet gasped.

He nodded, "Xeno-1 is more erratic, one of my samples has even died! Even the electromagnetic field between samples seems weaker. We will need to test the fragments you brought back and check my results on new samples but this is a very promising beginning!"

"It worked." Jaspreet could hardly believe it. All of that walking, her injury, everything was worth it.

*   *   *

Jaspreet was leaning against the counter, her eyes closed, unmindful of her exposed leg or of anything really. A soft smile graced her full lips but a clear sense of exhaustion kept her glued to her chair more than the two soldiers manning the door to the lab.

Jason pressed the start button for the first test he was conducting on the fragments of the lattice and then turned to look at a different shard through a microscope.

"Dr. Scordato!" Someone called out from between the watching soldiers.

Jason jerked away from the microscope, "Hmm?"

"It's Agatha, she's collapsed." Jason's brain caught hold of the information and his body lurched into motion without ever registering who the speaker was.

"Agatha." He rushed to the door. His mind raced miles ahead of his body. He had to see Agatha, check her vitals, see if she would recover.

The soldiers at the door began to block his path. "Move." Jason commanded, finding his voice more self-assured than he thought possible.

They hesitated but as he continued to walk toward them, they slipped aside so his passage wouldn't touch them. Jason ignored how their fingers twitched beside their guns.

The hallway stretched out before him. With some effort he made his way through the halls at a normal, if sped up gait. He went through the maze of cots with that same swiftness heedless of the innumerable number of beds he ricocheted off in his haste.

"Dr. Scodato!" A voice cried out, the man who Jason vaguely recognized as one of the new soldiers stood from his chair and gently directed Jason to take his place. Jason glanced at the man just long enough to nod his thanks and then his attention reverted entirely back to Agatha.

Her head tilted oddly to the side, allowing her mouth to hang open. Someone had draped a blanket over her and tucked it around her in a cocoon. Jason leaned forward and rummaged under the blanket, finally finding and grasping one cold, thin hand. He felt for her pulse. His own heart stopped, every inch of him stilling as he focused on feeling any movement in his friends' veins. He shifted his fingers slightly, searching.

Finally, he felt it, a thin reedy pulse, so slow as to be nearly gone. But still identifiably there. Jason felt tears prick at his eyes and he leaned forward, his forehead resting on the blanketed edge of her bed. His fingers stayed locked on her pulse.

16

Treegar watched Dr. Scordato lean over, his head coming to rest on Agatha's bed and his hand gripping her wrist. It felt voyeuristic to stand there, seeing their intimacy and yet know she wasn't part of it. She pulled back, looking away and moving further into the kitchen area, her eyes glancing over the table, remembering the shock as Agatha collapsed.

The sound of pounding feet drew her focus across the room to Lieutenant Ward as he marched in flanked by several soldiers. None of whom she recognized from her own squad.

"Scordato!" Ward stopped several paces away from Agatha's bed, the soldiers spreading out around him. They kept their hands off of their weapons but their posture was one of anticipation.

"What's going on here, Lieutenant?" Garner took a step forward, imposing his body slightly between Scordato and Ward's men.

"That is none of your concern, Corporal. Dr. Scordato presents a security risk and needs to be dealt with."

Treegar raised an eyebrow. The doctor looked like a strong wind would topple him right now, what sort of risk could he pose to anyone? Her skin prickled. Has he been infected? Her heart stuttered and she glanced between Scordato's hunched form, Garner, and Ward.

Garner leaned down and shook Scordato's shoulder. Treegar took a step forward, her mouth opening too late to prevent the action.

"Hmm?" Scordato grunted, looking up.

Treegar's mouth felt like sandpaper. Garner motioned with his chin at the group facing them and Scordato's head turned to follow Garner's gaze. His shoulders tensed when he saw what faced him.

"How can I help you?" Treegar almost missed Scordato's question, posed so softly it was less than a whisper. She exhaled in relief. He wasn't infected.

She tore her eyes from Scordato's back and looked at Ward. His jaw was tense and his eyes had a hard, flint-like quality. They held a fear within them that Scordato's question hadn't been erased. "You need to leave. You and everyone who has touched you or Dr. Nagi since her… accident."

Scordato shook his head, "What? Why? You can see for yourself that I'm not infected."

Ward shook his own head, "We don't know that. We don't know what will happen. I can't risk this community for you."

Scordato shook his head. Treegar tensed as she parsed Ward's words. Anyone who had touched Scordato would be cast out too. Garner. She felt a sudden flush of anger. Ward had stood and watched as Garner touched Scordato and he had said nothing, only throwing down judgement after the fact.

Her hand twitched, if she had been wearing her gun, she would have shot Ward in that moment. She didn't doubt that she would have quickly followed him as his guards would shoot her in turn, but if it allowed Garner to stay here it would be worth it.

Garner lifted his hand, looked at it and then back at Ward. "What are you talking about?" he cried out.

"You heard me. You, Dr. Scordato, Dr. Nagi, Agatha and anyone else you four have touched since Dr. Nagi was injured, need to leave. We can't risk having you here."

"Why? None of us are infected. This makes no sense!"

Treegar saw Ward harden his stance, the muscles in his jaw twitching. "Nagi was injured by a piece of the meteorite, we have no idea how it is going to affect her. You think I should do what he did and risk everyone here by allowing someone who could kill us all to remain here?"

"What are you talking about?" Garner demanded.

"Agatha." Scordato croaked. "She wasn't infected."

"We didn't know that. She could have been an asymptomatic carrier; you could be too. You might be willing to risk the lives of my men, but I'm not. Pack a bag and get out."

Scordato dropped Agatha's hand, the limb falling limp on to her chest. "She wasn't a carrier. We ran tests. You could do the same. This is just an excuse to get rid of us." His shoulders drooped a little bit more at the hard expression on Ward's face. "I'll go. I won't fight you. Agatha's gone. She's gone." It looked like his strength abandoned him and he pitched forward on to Agatha's corpse and wept.

Treegar swallowed. The doctor's grief filled the air. Even Ward had the decency to look uncomfortable.

Garner looked back at Treegar, his face soft and his eyes calling to her. Madison was captivated by that look, her heart swelling and her throat constricting. He opened his mouth and then snapped it shut, doubt clouding his eyes.

He turned to look at Scordato and then Ward, "I guess I'll go pack."

Treegar's chest constricted painfully. He couldn't leave her here! She stepped forward and announced, "I'm going too."

"No," Garner snapped, "you haven't touched anyone. You need to stay here."

Madison clenched her jaw and reached out to touch Garner. He pulled back, leaving her hand hanging in the air. "I'm going with you." She took another step forward, he stepped back. She didn't reach for him a second time. This time she crouched beside Dr. Scordato and gave him a side hug. Pressing into him and leveraging him up from Agatha's body. "Come on, they won't let us take forever packing. If she's gone, then there's nothing left for you to do."

Scordato swallowed noisily and sniffed. "Her rings. She wanted her daughters to get her rings. I… I promised." His voice was thick and soft.

"I understand." Madison said and then released his shoulders to lean down and check Agatha's hands for rings. The hand closest, which Jason had so recently been grasping was bare but the one opposite had two large gold rings on her second to last finger. They sat loosely around her bones, kept on by her swollen knuckles. Madison tried to ease them over the knuckle but they were stuck. She gritted her teeth and worked them back and forth, the papery skin wearing under her efforts. Finally, with a silent pop, they rounded the thickness of the knuckle and were free.

She released a shuddering sigh. The rings that looked too big on Agatha's skeletal hand looked dainty in her own palm. She placed the hand on top of the other on Agatha's chest.

Everyone was watching her. Treegar avoided looking into anyone's face and held the rings out to Scordato. He extended his palm and she dropped the rings into it. "Let's get going." She turned and marched to her bunk.

*   *   *

"And it doesn't bother you that you might be condemning the scientists who stopped this threat to an icy death?" Jaspreet argued with Ward even as she was herded down the corridor by soldiers she had thought about as friends.

"If what you did worked, then you won't meet with any

surprises. Just find yourself a nice shelter and hunker down like the rest of us. But you and I know that that's a pretty big if. Don't you think it is smarter for me to protect those I can?"

Jaspreet glanced at Jason. He dragged his feet, his pack hanging down from one shoulder and his eyes glazed while two soldiers prodded him into motion every other step. Jaspreet had to admit he didn't look good. The shock and grief of Agatha's death and this sudden turn by Ward had really done a number on him. She could understand Ward's distrust of her injury but other than being tired and hungry she was fine. His distrust didn't explain why he was kicking Jason and the other two soldiers out as well.

The woman's helmet was already on, visor pulled down obscuring her face. The male soldier looked like he was grinding his teeth together as the muscles in his jaw twitched and he glared at Ward. They both carried themselves like they were ready for a fight.

At the end of the corridor stood two more soldiers, geared up and standing to either side of an oblong bundle. Ropes had been tied around the bundle to secure what Jaspreet could tell were sheets and the soldiers each held a connected rope with one hand while keeping their weapons trained on the bundle.

"What is this?" Jaspreet demanded.

"I said everyone the two of you touched and I meant it. Agatha goes with you." Ward ordered and his men shifted their guns toward her to underline his words.

Jason stiffened and looked at Ward. For a moment Jaspreet couldn't see Jason's face but the side of Ward's jaw twitched before Jason looked away and walked toward the soldier to the right of the Agatha and the door. The soldier dropped the rope and sidestepped out of the way before Jason reached him.

Jason bent down and retrieved the rope. He began pulling, Agatha's shrouded body barely budging even as he leaned his entire body into the task. The male soldier slid his helmet on and took a step forward but even as he moved the woman was faster. In a series of quick steps she moved to the other waiting soldier and scooped the second lead rope from his hand. He scrambled back and she moved past him and leaned her weight to the task. Agatha began to slide.

Jaspreet looked back at Ward. She hoped her hatred and contempt were clear in her face. Her eyes felt hard and her lips were pressed together in a harsh line. Ward's face softened for an instant before he looked down, unable to hold her gaze.

A soldier behind him held out a small bag, "This goes too. I don't want it here anymore." Ward took the bag and tossed it at her feet. Jaspreet bent down and picked it up, keeping her eyes on Ward and the surrounding soldiers as she did.

"There are no villains here, Dr. Nagi. Just people trying to protect people. Go. I bear you no ill will, but I cannot risk having you here."

Jaspreet straightened and spat on the floor, "You tell yourself that if it helps you sleep at night, but you and I both know you're just looking for an excuse to get rid of us." She turned and marched out the door. She kept her shoulders square and her head high despite the sudden buffeting of arctic winds and the slanting glare of the sun reflecting off snow.

17

Jason leaned into the rope. His legs shook under him, but he channeled his body's desire to collapse into pulling the rope. His mind shied away from what he was dragging behind him.

The soldier who walked beside him was blessedly silent, simply matching their steps to his. The snow crunched under his boots, barely lit by the lingering twilight.

Night had fallen so slowly he had barely noticed, only the increased strain on his eyes made an impression. He slipped and his knees gave out, throwing him into the ice-hardened snow pack. His hands remained locked on the rope, frozen to their task, and his shoulder and helmet hit the ground first in a jarring thud.

He lay there as the cold seeped through the protective gear and gnawed at his skin. His visor fogged from his laboured breath. His mind detached from his body, floating in a numb abyss. *Was this what death felt like? Is this what Agatha felt?*

Then hands grabbed him and rolled him over, shook him and voices shouted at him. His mind tried to translate the sounds into something recognizable, but it felt like he was wading through sludge. The sounds made no sense. His body was distant and the sounds grew further and further away. His eyes rolled up into his head and everything went black.

*　　　*　　　*

"We have to stop here. We can't drag two bodies and Scordato's out cold," Garner advised.

Treegar nodded and swung her pack off her back to pull out the small tent and bedroll that comprised most of its contents. It took only a few practiced movements for her to shake it out and begin setting it up. It would be a tight fit for the four of them, but the close quarters would keep them warm and she doubted that either scientist had the presence of mind to pack their own shelter.

Garner helped her drive the pegs into the snow to keep the corners down and then she helped him drag Dr. Scordato inside. Dr. Nagi dragged herself in behind them and closed the tent door. Treegar rolled out her bedroll and everyone collapsed on to some portion of it. After a moment's rest, Garner pulled out his own and threw it over the scientists.

"I'll take the first watch," he offered.

Treegar nodded and settled herself next to Dr. Nagi. They hadn't traveled far but she knew that she needed to grab some rest before it was her turn on watch. Her stomach growled and her shoulder bit uncomfortably into the hard packed snow. But those discomforts faded away as she forced her consciousness into the drifting tide of sleep.

*   *   *

"…Don't know what they found. They couldn't have completed the tests. Superstitious idiot, didn't even wait for an actual answer."

"Doesn't matter now, we have it."

"Are you sure it won't hurt us?"

"As sure as I can be about something I don't actually understand. It never hurt anyone at the lab and I was injured by a piece of it breaking and hitting me, not from any weird alien power. It's not even that heavy, I can carry it. Besides, I'd hate to just leave it in the wilderness. Not if we could still learn something from it."

"Fine, so long as you don't think it will be a problem."

Jason tried to parse the conversation he was hearing but everything felt distant and foggy. The voices kept coming, never stopping long enough for his mind to catch up.

"Where do you think we should go now?"

"South. Winter will hold up here for at least another month. We won't survive out here if we are picking at the same supplies as the Base. And I have a bad feeling that if they find us out here they will have orders to shoot on sight."

"You don't think they actually would?" Jason finally placed the voice as that belonging to Dr. Nagi, Jaspreet.

"I absolutely think they would. Some might think first, but we can't risk our lives on that. It's best to get gone."

Jason shifted. His legs ached. Despite the inviting oblivion his body began to lodge several increasingly urgent complaints and with those complaints came confusion regarding a multitude of things. Where was he? Why were the voices worried about being shot? Why were they moving south?

"We need to leave Agatha."

"Nnnn!" Jason felt like a bucket of cold water had been tossed on him. He jerked and shouted in protest, the sound and movement both less controlled than he intended. His arms flailed and his legs twitched, sending a spasm of pain through his nerves. "Ahh!" He moaned.

"You're awake!" Jaspreet exclaimed.

Jason forced his eyes open and tried to communicate again. "No." He met Jaspreet's confused look and swallowed. He needed to be clearer. "We can't leave her." It came out as a plea and Jaspreet recognized it as such. She smiled, although it was thin and forced, nothing like her usual broad grin.

"We can't leave her." He repeated. His mind is still sifting through the memories and puzzle pieces that led him to this moment.

"We have no choice." The voice to Jason's left answered. It was male, and familiar, Jason tried to place it.

"There is always a choice." Jason turned his head to look at the man, his name finally popping into his mind, "Corporal Garner."

"Well, in this case the choice is between dragging a dead woman behind us and all of us dying or burying her in the snow here and maybe, just maybe, we live."

It couldn't be as simple as that. Jason pressed his lips together and struggled through his muddle mind for an answer, he couldn't just abandon Agatha like this.

Jaspreet placed a gloved hand over Jason's, "I'm afraid Garner is right. We should give her a decent burial here. She doesn't deserve to be dragged further." Her tone was compassionate but final.

Jason shook his head, scrambling his brains further. Agatha deserved to be returned to her family. She deserved a decent burial, not some nameless grave in the snow that would melt in a few months and expose her to the ravages of wild animals.

A second soldier moved from behind Jaspreet, leaning forward and then crawling out of the tent. Icy winter air slipped into their place, biting at Jason and sending shivers across his body.

Garner reached into his bag and pulled out a bar. He unwrapped part of it and offered it to Jason, "You need to eat something."

Jason numbly accepted the bar and looked at it. It consisted of pressed dried fruit and nuts. The sight both nauseated him and made his stomach clench uncomfortably with hunger. He pushed up the visor on his helmet and tested the corner of it in his mouth. It was sweet and hard. His teeth worked through the corner successfully separating a morsel. His tongue worked on the piece, sucking the sweetness of it and swallowing.

Garner closed his bag and began folding and rolling the blanket that was draped over Jason. Jason shifted to release a corner of it that was trapped under his left leg. Jaspreet left the tent, letting another icy blast inside. Jason sat up and worked at the corner of the bar until Garner was finished stuffing the blanket into the top of a pack.

"Here." Garner said, dropping the bag beside Jason, "This is yours."

Jason nodded and swallowed to make a reply, but Garner had already turned to leave.

Jason looked morosely at the backpack and then at the barely nibbled fruit and nut bar. How could they even think about leaving Agatha? The thought made his stomach churn and he hastily covered the bar in the opened wrapper and shoved it into a side pocket of the bag.

He took a deep breath, focusing for a moment on finalizing his thoughts. His mind finally felt clear again. With considerable gentleness he eased himself up into a kneeling position and hefted the bag onto his back. It was heavy enough to nearly overbalance him but he caught himself with his left hand. He crawled to the tent opening and took another deep breath of relatively warm air before flipping his visor back into place and opening the flap.

Cold air hit him like a slap and nearly drove him back into the tent. Jason forced himself forward. He needed to convince them to bring Agatha. They couldn't leave her, they just couldn't.

The world was shrouded in pre-dawn light, stars twinkling above unhindered by the brilliance of the moon. The snow had a bluish cast, reflecting the skies' grandeur.

Agatha's body was a dark smudge on the snow. A black slug

at the end of a long, meandering trail that disappeared into the distance. Jason stood, half upright, half crouched, staring at the bundle. Frost glistened around the edges, clinging to the crisscrossing ropes which tied the blankets in place and adding an otherworldly and fuzzy quality to it.

The sound of scraping broke the silence, pulling Jason's focus from Agatha to the right of the tent. Garner, Jaspreet, and the other soldier were using sticks and their hands to dig. Jason started, his heart stuttering to a stop in his chest.

"No." He sobbed. The sound traveled no further than the breath it fogged on the inside of his visor. "No." He declared louder.

Jaspreet looked up from her digging but the two soldiers kept going.

Jason took a half step toward them, stumbling, his legs nearly giving out. "You can't!" He yelled. Tears blurred his vision.

Arms caught him and held him up, pulling him close. "Shh… I'm sorry." Jaspreet whispered into the side of his head. "I'm sorry. It's the only option."

"No…" Jason sobbed again, clinging to her but wishing he could push her away. Push them all away.

She held him until his knees gave out and he sank into the snow. She let him collapse then, easing his journey but no longer able to support his dead weight. She returned to the digging. They dug until the first rays of sunlight crested the snow. Jason mutely staring on, all arguments against their actions dying in his frozen throat.

The two soldiers pulled the ropes out of the frozen snow where they had been dropped and ripped Agatha from where she had rested that night. The frozen shroud wrapped corpse slid over the snow and slipped into the hand dug grave while pinks and golds slashed across the sky.

Jaspreet nudged Jason, "You should say something." She urged.

Jason swallowed. What could he say to the woman whose last months he had stolen? Who had become a friend and companion through the most terrifying time of his life? He took a shuddering breath and tried, "Agatha Abernathy…"

He paused, tears clouding his vision and despite the winter wind his face felt unnaturally hot. "Agatha was an incredible woman. Illness that would have debilitated most didn't prevent her from seeking the truth. She showed me," His voice broke with a sob and it took him several long wracking moments before he had control over his body and his voice once again, "She showed me more than I can ever really put into words. She was strong, kind, and wise. The world is a darker place for her passing from it." His voice trailed off.

The four of them stood there for a long minute of silence and then Jaspreet approached Agatha, bent down and lifted a fistful of snow and dropped it on to her. "May she rest in peace."

"Amen." Garner's voice softly agreed. Then he and the other soldier began pushing the piles of snow around the grave over Agatha. the pristine white splashing against the blanket that covered her and reflected the light in a prism of colour. The lightest of powder puffed into the air, catching the early dawn light and creating rainbows.

Jason stared as the last sign of Agatha was obscured by snow. All too soon all that remained was a mound of shifted snow in a vast winter landscape.

Jaspreet knelt beside him long after the soldiers had finished and left. He could hear them dismantling the tent but his body refused to leave that spot. He couldn't leave Agatha in this unmarked grave in the middle of nowhere. It felt disrespectful. It felt diminishing. She deserved a monument, something permanent, something that yelled to the world "she was here!" But he had nothing to give. The snow obscured even the rocks that he might have piled up to her in a simple cairn.

All too soon the soldiers were done packing away the tent. Jaspreet pulled at his arm, "It's time to go," She murmured.

Jason resisted but his will quickly gave way and he allowed her to pull him up. The sun rose as he and Jaspreet followed the soldiers away from the base.

18

It felt unmoored. Loosed in a manner heretofore unimagined. Something unknown that had held a piece of the virus was suddenly missing. It floundered among the minds that were it. But now it sensed that it had been more. That an ancient piece had been torn away. Left only the minds and bodies of those it infected, the virus was suddenly aware of them in an intimate manner. It was overwhelming. Hunger. Pain. Fever. Concepts which had been foreign were now real. It released a scream, a howl, a screech, a moan of confusion and pain. Billions of throats voiced its agony.

*   *   *

Charissa coached Sophia and Atticus through the phonetic alphabet. Penelope and Timothy were taking a nap and the kids were tired of watching TV and being quiet all the time. Linguistics was a good distraction as both kids thought that the strange sounds some of the letters made were funny.

"I want to!" Penelope's voice carried through the hall.

Oh no, Charissa thought, *not another fight.* They had barely made up from the last one. Timothy seemed pretty shaken up by Luna and hadn't wanted to go back out the next day, or the day after, and Charissa didn't want to push the issue since he and Penelope were finally talking again.

She couldn't make out Timothy's reply but figured that the kids needed a more engaging distraction than just her. "Hey kids, want to watch a video about linguistics? Maybe we can learn some ancient Egyptian?" Charissa clicked over to YouTube and began searching for the video she had in mind.

"I can already speak Egyptian!" Sophia declared.

"Oh really?"

"Yup! It's all bird, eye, person, bird. I saw pictures!"

Atticus looked suitably impressed by his sister's knowledge.

Charissa smiled, "Those are actually called Hieroglyphs and they don't actually mean bird, eye, and person. Each picture is actually a word. Here watch this video and you'll see what I mean." She clicked play, skipped the ad, and the video began.

The clear voice of the video covered the muted voices of Timothy and Penelope's argument. In the middle of the video her phone buzzed with an incoming message. Flipping it over and checking the screen revealed Ryosuke's name and the first few words.

"Who's Rrroosuk?" Sophia asked, struggling through the name.

"It's Ryosuke." Charissa clarified, sounding the name out slowly so her niece could catch the proper pronunciation. "And he's a friend."

"Is he your boyfriend?" Atticus giggled.

Charissa shook her head, "No, just a friend?"

"Is he smelly?" Sophia asked.

Charissa chuckled, "No, at least I don't think so. I might be the smelly one. I don't really know him all that well. Now shh, you're missing the video."

Thankfully the kids responded to her redirection and left her to actually open and read Ryosuke's message.

*   *   *

"Okay, what's going on?" Charissa asked once Penelope emerged from her bedroom.

Penelope glanced at the kids and shrugged, "Later."

At Charissa's skeptical eyebrow, Penelope assured, "I promise."

Sophia turned and looked at her mother, "What do you promise Mommy?"

Penelope widened her eyes and flattened her lips at Charissa before instantly shifting into a guileless smile when she looked at her daughter. "I promised Aunt Charry that I'm going to teach her to crochet. You two want to help?"

"Yeah!" Both kids exclaimed and then raced each other to grab Penelope's yarn bag.

Charissa rolled her eyes and sighed, at least this would keep them busy for a few hours as the kids made knots, undid them, rolled balls, and maybe made a few chains.

Penelope patiently worked with Charissa to chain and begin working on a scarf. It never looked difficult when Penelope did it but Charissa's fingers seemed to fumble the yarn and make it twist and tangle in the strangest ways. By the time the kids were done with the activity Charissa had a long lumpy chain into which she had been trying to squeeze a series of single crochet stitches back into.

Penelope ushered the kids into their play room to tear it apart and then returned.

"Where's Timothy?" Charissa prodded.

Penelope tilted her head and returned to her chair, "Sulking."

Charissa raised her eyebrow.

"I want to go on a supply run. I need to get out of the house and I need to know what's out there." Penelope confessed.

"Oh." That was probably the last thing Charissa expected to hear. She honestly hadn't thought Penelope had any desire to leave this place especially after the fight it took for her to agree to the little supply run that Charissa and Timothy went on a few days ago.

"When you and Tim were out there… I was out of my mind with worry. I have no idea what you faced out there. Tim told me some of it, about Luna. All I can do is imagine and that seems somehow so much worse than knowing."

"Oh," Charissa repeated and then cleared her throat, "Um, that makes sense. You've never seen what it does to them, have you?"

Penelope shook her head, "Only in videos and on TV. Maybe it's stupid to feel this way, but…"

"But you need to see it for yourself. Timothy and I have both seen them and now you, I don't know, maybe you feel left out?"

"No, that isn't it. I think… I think that I feel unprepared. How can I protect Sophia and Atticus, or even you or Tim, if I have no idea the reality of what I'm facing? What if there comes a day where I need to protect you guys but I freeze when I see one of those things cause I've never seen one before?

Charissa bit her lip, that sounded like Penelope had really thought about this.

"Well, I want to go on another run. Just next door, to grab the stuff we couldn't get last time. Maybe you and I could do that tomorrow. If anything happens Timothy is right here and we can run on back. It might be scary but at least we know more or less what to expect."

Penelope gave her a weak smile, "Thanks. I'd like that. Or, well, I appreciate it. You know what I mean."

Charissa laughed softly, "Come on, let's go tell your husband. I'm sure this is really going to endear me to him but whatever."

*   *   *

"Please don't do this." Timothy whispered to Penelope.

Charissa turned her head and focused on putting her rubber boots on.

"We've talked about this. I'm doing it. It'll be fine. I'll be right back." Penelope stated calmly.

Charissa gave them another moment but her boots were firmly on and finally she gave up and stood. Timothy was staring at Penelope, his lips pressed together and his eyes full of concern. Penelope was checking her gear and ensuring everything was fastened properly. Charissa turned and started to double check Penelope.

"Make sure you come back." Timothy whispered.

"I will." Penelope promised.

With both of them checked and double checked the two sisters prepared to step outside. Charissa turned to knob and paused before cracking the door open a millimetre.

The space in front of the door looked the same as it had when she and Timothy returned from their brief trip. While the early sunlight left some deep shadows the street and front lawn looked free of any movement, even many of the previously twitching creatures had stilled.

She eased the door open further and slipped out, Penelope a half step behind. The half frozen, rotting animals that littered the steps and yard revolted Charissa but required nothing more than a cursory glance to reassure herself that they were no longer trying to move.

Charissa led the way around the house and through the gate to the neighbours' yard. Luna was a dark, bloated lump waiting for them. When the mass shifted Charissa hurried her steps past it and to the deck.

The transition of light from the early morning to the interior barely slowed their progress. Charissa scanned the interior and led them straight to the kitchen where the cupboards were still open from their last visit. "Take what's left." She directed Penelope, taking up the position that Timothy had previously held.

Penelope swung her bag down and began filling it with canned goods. Charissa remained peripherally aware of her sister while focusing on their surroundings, watching for any sign of change or movement. Long tense moments passed where the only discernible sounds came from Penelope as she stacked cans and boxes into her bag. "Full. Give me yours." Charissa slipped the straps down and handed her bag to Penelope and then accepted the full bag, shrugging it on and pulling her gun back into position.

Something clicked. Charissa's head snapped to face the backyard.

A gunshot rent the air.

Charissa and Penelope huddled backward, crouching into the corner of the kitchen. Penelope scrambled to lift her rifle into readiness and Charissa strained to regain control of her now racing heart.

The steps creaked.

"Stay back!" Charissa croaked. "Stay back!" She tried again and the steps ceased.

"Hello?" a masculine voice called out.

"Is someone there?" A woman's voice asked.

Charissa glanced nervously at Penelope. "Who is it?" Her voice was clearer and steadier. At least they now knew whoever was approaching wasn't infected though as she thought about it the gun shot itself had given that away.

"Woah! There are people here!" A different male voice exclaimed.

Charissa cursed, whoever was out there clearly outnumbered

them.

"Just some folks." The first voice called out in answer to her question. "Just some folks looking for supplies. You live here?" A tall figure stepped into the doorway to the kitchen.

Charissa straightened up and adjusted her rifle. "No, just getting supplies. Same as you."

The figure stopped and raised their hands. They were dressed in a mishmash of plastic clothing, yellow rain pants, a blackish jacket, Halloween serial killer mask, black boots and a cowboy hat. A hunting rifle hanging loosely in their right hand. "You were here first, I respect that. We aren't looking for trouble. It's just been a while since we encountered anyone else. Wouldn't mind swapping some stories, if you're interested?" He gestured to the table and chairs off to the side of the kitchen.

Against the advice of her pounding heart, Charissa lowered her weapon and nodded. Neither she nor Penelope were prepared for any kind of fight with these people, talking sounded like a better plan. "Don't have much." She cautioned. She and Penelope sidled over to the table.

The man moved toward the table with a fluid grace that reminded Charissa of a wolf. "I'm Randy. Outside are Mallory and Ryosuke."

Charissa's ears perked up, "Ryosuke?"

"Yeah, you know him?" There was surprise evident in Randy's voice.

"He saved me a while back." She confessed.

"Heh!" Randy laughed, "That sounds like Ryosuke. Hey Ryosuke, got one of your rescues in here!"

Another figure stepped into the door frame; this one wearing a ski mask. "Oh, yeah?" He asked and then took a few steps closer to Charissa and Penelope.

Charissa lifted the stepped visor on her welding shield, exposing her face to the chilly morning air. "Hey," she greeted before flipping it back down.

"Charissa?" Ryosuke exclaimed, "Oh that's right, you live around here, don't you?"

"Yeah," Charissa nodded.

"Cool! Is this your sister?"

"Yeah." Charissa didn't know if she felt more or less comfortable with Ryosuke being one of these people. On one hand he was nice and had rescued her at the start of this whole thing. On the other hand, they knew where she and Penelope lived, even just approximately, and knowing that they were out looking for supplies she wasn't comfortable with that.

"Good to see you!" There was a genuine note to his voice that almost made Charissa smile despite her nerves.

"Good to see you too. How's your research going? What have you been up to?" She asked reflexively.

Ryosuke waved his arms in a vague gesture around him, his rifle swinging wide as he did so. "Just what you see, surviving, not much more I can do right now."

"No progress on your theories?"

He shrugged, "Not yet. For now, they remain just theories. Don't have a lot of resources. Been following the science as much as I can. Did you read that stuff that Dr. Fox leaked? I sent you the link, crazy right?"

"Yeah, crazy. I, uh, I've been learning more about linguistics. You know, just in case, wanna be ready and all."

"That's too cool! Way to go!"

"Yeah." Charissa lapsed into silence.

"Well, it's nice to see you."

"Same." It was nice to see him. Even if she couldn't see his face through the mask.

"Well… alright then." Randy interjected. "Glad that's over. So, what news did you get? Which houses have you cleaned out? Any other monsters, like the one outside, that we should know about?"

Charissa opened her mouth to lie and say they'd cleared out most of this block, when the unknown woman's voice called from outside.

"Guy's! Get out here, somethings happening!"

Ryosuke and Randy scrambled out of the house in a flurry of movement while Charissa and Penelope hung back.

"What should we do?" Penelope whispered.

"Grab the supplies and then let's get out of here. Try not to let them know which house is ours." Dang, she wished Timothy was here instead of either her or Penelope, at least he was big and intimidating. She'd be less worried about them knowing where they lived if they had a reason to leave them alone.

Penelope grabbed the bag, zipped it up, and slung it on to her back. "Let's see what's happening."

Ryosuke, Randy and someone who must be Mallory stood outside the house silently listening. The hairs on Charissa's arms raised and she hung back with Penelope, her gun readied just in case. But as they all stood in silence a faint but persistent wail reached their ears. Charissa could barely make it out but it made her whole body break out into a cold sweat.

The trio looked around the yard as though they expected an immediate attack. They moved so their backs were facing each other and their weapons were out ready for whatever might come. Slowly they made their way out of the yard and disappeared behind the building.

Charissa shuddered and tried to make her body move. The horrible cry grew louder till it filled her mind with fear. Her knees nearly crumpled beneath her, she only recovered by using their collapse to propel her forward, Penelope drifting in her wake. They edged past the corpse of Luna and trekked to their front door in a haze of primal fear.

Her mind was so clouded by the sound that they were in the foyer before Charissa could even wonder where it was coming from.

19

Gone was strategy, gone was reason. Only the hunger and the drive remained. The virus swam through its minds, the echoing loss continuing to alert it periodically of what it once was.

*   *   *

"INFECTED ACROSS NORTH AMERICA HAVE BEGUN TO MAKE NOISE AND EAT VICTIMS. THE SUDDEN CHANGE IN BEHAVIOUR AND AGGRESSION HAS AUTHORITIES SCRAMBLING. AS USUAL THE BEST THING YOU CAN DO FOR YOURSELF AND YOUR FAMILY IS TO REMAIN AT HOME. DO NOT GO OUTSIDE. AUTHORITIES ASSURE US THAT THEY ARE WORKING DILIGENTLY TO GAIN CONTROL OVER THE SITUATION." The Newscaster worked hard to keep their fear out of their voice but they couldn't control the pallor of their face or the sheen of terror in their eyes.

Greg suppressed a shudder. The screeching moan of the infected lay under the voice of the newscaster. The rending sound sent the hairs on his neck up and elicited a fear which was hard to suppress.

He rubbed his face with both hands, trying to remove the permanently crusty feel in his eyes.

"Sir," An aide entered his office at a speed that was just shy of a run, "There's been another development."

Greg dropped his hands and looked up, "What now?"

"Japan and China have reported attacks."

His heart stuttered and he mentally grasped at the straws of his composure. "Thank you." He muttered from years of habit, although he realized as soon as the words were out that it was insane to thank someone for such dire, world ending news. It had spread. Barriers of water had been conquered and now it was only a matter of time before it reached the whole world.

"Sir, how is research on the cure going?"

Greg shook his head, unable to force his throat to verbally squash their hope. After Ward's report of an accident in the primary lab and the loss of doctors Scordato and Nagi, what little progress they might have been making was now gone. The cure would not, could not, be ready in time to save humanity.

*   *   *

At one point in his life Jason had fancied himself something of an athlete. Not on the level of a professional, but maybe a talented amateur. He had played soccer, basketball, and run track, but that was a lifetime ago. Now, trudging through the snow, with icy air slipping through every thin spot or break in his attire, he felt every single one of his years. He was no longer a young man, and hadn't been one for some time.

Two days. Two days of walking. One to bury Agatha and one more into their journey south. In the endlessly white landscape, time and movement were meaningless. All Jason knew was the impetus to place one foot in front of the other.

They stopped for food and water. The soldiers kept an eye on the surrounding snow while Jason and Jaspreet sank to the ground. If he hadn't been so tired, he would have wept. From pain, from exhaustion, from grief. He drank melted snow and chewed the small amount of food he was given without thought, without attachment, and without commitment.

Then the journey continued. He needed help getting up from where he had fallen. A strong gloved hand clasped him and hauled him up like a sack of potatoes. He was too enveloped in his own fog to even register which soldier helped him. With automatic obedience he took his place in line behind Jaspreet and began marching.

They walked on, the two soldiers switching positions periodically, breaking a line through the snow. Creating a slash through the pristine landscape which came from nothing and led toward nothing. When the light dimmed, the soldiers halted and set up the tent. Jason's fog wrapped him in a thick grey blanket, keeping all emotions, fatigue, and even pain from his mind.

Once the tent was set up Jason crawled inside and passed out.

*   *   *

"He's not doing well." Garner observed. He munched on his portion of their meager supplies and watched the sleeping doctor.

"Is he sick?" Treegar asked. She kept a cautious eye on the man while devouring her own portion of what they were calling dinner that day. It consisted of little more than a few strips of dried fruit which she had to work to break down before washing it down with a small sip of water from her canteen. She wasn't producing enough saliva to break the fruit down on her own, a clear sign of dehydration so she drank more deeply from her supply.

"More likely exhausted and grieving. Though we should check his feet for blisters, all of this walking won't be doing him any favors. How are you holding up?" He questioned Dr. Nagi.

She shook her head and indicated that she needed a moment. After taking a sip from her own canteen and swallowing hard, she replied, "I'm fine. I'm holding up. I'll need to check my leg at some point and change the bandage but it can wait." Her voice was a rough whisper.

Garner nodded, "Let us know if anything changes. We are in this together. I'm hoping that we can find more supplies before we encounter any opposition. You and Scordato are going to need more calories if you have to keep up in a fight. I hope we find a hunting lodge or something, somewhere with guns. The least Ward could have done was let us bring our guns."

"Might as well be naked out here." Treegar observed. "But why send guns out with dead men?"

The landscape they had been moving through held a ridiculous dream-like quality. Endless hills of snow leading to more hills of snow. There were smudges on the horizon that might indicate either trees or buildings. Treegar hoped that they would reach them tomorrow. If only that there was a chance of more food and better shelter.

"Check your wound in the morning. For now, rest." Garner ordered looking first at Dr. Nagi and then at Treegar.

Treegar nodded and took another drink from her canteen before closing it and settling down. Garner shifted in beside her. Since that first night they hadn't bothered with watches during the night. You couldn't see anything, it was bone shatteringly cold, and if there was something out there, with no guns, you couldn't do anything except tell everyone to run.

The tent warmed up rapidly as the four bodies settled into the limited floor space. Treegar allowed Garner's warmth to soak into her back, relaxing the muscles and chipping away at the ice in her core.

*   *   *

The next day was more of the same. Walking. Breaking trail. Slowly making their way toward the smudges. Step by step they grew, until the quartet topped a hill and suddenly there it was, a small cabin nestled among a windbreak of trees.

Once they could clearly see their destination, each member of the group picked up the pace, eating through the remaining distance.

"Hold." Garner ordered quietly, "We don't know what we might find. I need you two," he indicated the doctors, "to stay outside and alert us if you see any movement. Treegar and I will ascertain if it is safe." He moved forward with smooth, stealthy movements.

Treegar fell in behind him. With the Doctors hobbling along in her wake.

Garner silently indicated for the doctors to take up positions on either side of the door and to face away from the building. He then tried the doorknob. It was locked. He nodded at Treegar and they both took a step back.

He rammed his shoulder into the door. The sound reverberated through the silence, amplified by the snow. The door held firm. He backed up and rammed it a second time, and then a third. On the fourth hit the area around the handle splintered. At the fifth it swung inward. Garner caught himself on the frame to keep from stumbling into the building.

Once he was righted, he began to creep inside. Treegar followed him, turning to keep her back and left side to him while she surveyed the right half of the cabin.

Nothing moved. The chill inside the building felt heavier than outside. Frost clung to the windows and sparkled on the furniture. No heat from the cold sun penetrated the walls.

Garner and Treegar advanced slowly into the building, moving as one creature. The main room of the cabin consisted of an entry way; with tile, a rug and an empty shoe rack; a sitting area and a small kitchen. Two doors led off from the main room and a set of stairs led to a second floor.

They explored the main area thoroughly before opening the first of the doors. They began with the one closest to the kitchen. It revealed a small bathroom with a shower, toilet and sink.

There were towels and toilet paper in a small wooden bookshelf between the toilet and sink.

The second door opened to a bedroom. A double bed was neatly made with a blue and green quilt and matching pillows. A cabinet stood at the end of the bed, empty except for a few hangers and a spare blanket.

With the main floor cleared, they proceeded up the stairs. The stairs opened into a loft under the roof. The room had two skylights that were covered in snow, allowing a whisper of blue light through. There was a large carpet and a queen-sized bed flanked with side tables and rustic lamps. A chest sat at the end of the bed with a grey blanket folded neatly on top.

A search of the chest only turned up more blankets and a few boardgames. The bedside tables were empty.

Treegar held back her frustration. Finding weapons had been a long shot, at least there were a few knives in the kitchen.

Treegar and Garner returned downstairs and called the doctors in. They both looked exhausted and nervous. Dr. Scordato gazed dully about the main room with little recognition, while Dr. Nagi looked longingly at the chairs.

Garner swung the door closed and then he and Treegar carried a side table to it and held it closed with that. "It looks like we are safe here for the moment." Garner announced.

Treegar noted how Dr. Nagi literally sagged at the pronouncement but Dr. Scordato seemed to not even hear it. Nagi moved to one of the chairs and sank into it. Scordato robotically copying her movements.

Treegar caught Garner's eye and made a quick motion with her chin toward Scordato. He nodded and took a step toward the doctors.

"Look, we can stay here for a day or so and rest. There isn't much in the way of supplies so we can't stay for longer than that. Besides, considering how little is between here and the base, we might want to keep moving anyway. I don't want to find out what will happen if our former friends find us while they are looking for supplies. There are a lot more of them than us, and they are much better armed."

The doctors looked defeated. Nagi looked like she might cry, but she didn't, instead she nodded and looked from Garner to Scordato. "At least we can rest for a bit. Jason, I'd like for you to check my leg."

Scordato nodded but made no effort to move.

"Is there a first aid kit or anything that I can use?" Nagi asked Garner and Treegar.

"Maybe in the bathroom." Garner suggested, pointing at the open door.

Dr. Nagi nodded, stood and made her way to the other room.

"I'll inventory our supplies." Treegar murmured to Garner. She had had enough spectating on wound maintenance while in the tent.

She moved to the kitchen and began pulling everything from the cupboards and piling them on the counter. Old, sturdy plates, bowls, and cups, cutlery, a can opener, and a few knives. Then the food, what there was of it: soup, canned pasta, an assortment of vegetables. No dried goods, which was probably what saved this place from being infested with infected rodents. Whoever this cabin belonged to hadn't left much of anything that might attract either vermin or robbers.

It wasn't much. Not even the knives, three in total. One, long and sharp but old. A medium length one that looked newer but felt duller. And a small paring knife with a wooden handle. Garner was right. They couldn't survive here for more than a few days. Four people and… she took a moment to count the cans, only 15 cans. Mixed with water, they could stretch it. But even then, they needed to keep moving. It would be stupid to stay here until they were completely out of food. They had no idea how far it would be till they found another building and had another opportunity to scavenge.

She returned to the main room, where Dr. Scordato was wrapping strips of towel around Dr. Nagi's thigh. Garner was visible in the main floor bedroom, setting his pack on the bed. Treegar chose to join him there.

"Hey." She greeted.

"How bad is it?" He asked.

"15 cans and three knives. Couple of butter knives if we want to count those."

Garner slumped on to the bed. "What have we gotten ourselves into, Madison?"

Treegar frowned and sat next to him, "I don't know." She swore.

"You shouldn't have come." Garner grumbled.

Treegar scoffed, "And leave you alone with the two doctors? You'd already be dead."

Garner barked a laugh, "hey, I think I would have gotten them this far at least."

"Sure, keep telling yourself that." She sighed, "besides, I couldn't stay there, not if they were the reason you were gone. It doesn't work like that, not for me."

Garner nudged her with his shoulder, "You're an idiot."

Treegar smiled, "Yeah, but so are you."

Garner stood and turned to look down at her, "Thank you. We should check on our ducklings." He held out his hand to her.

Treegar batted his hand away and stood on her own.

Garner grinned and preceded her out of the room and back into the main area.

Dr. Nagi was once again dressed, though her injured thigh was noticeably thicker than her other one. "Could we do something to warm this place up?" She asked.

"We could light a fire, but I don't see any firewood. Want to explore outside with me to see if we can find any? There might be a shed on the other side of the building."

Dr. Nagi's shoulders slumped but she nodded. With a sigh, she stood up and followed Garner to the door. Together they slid the side table out of the way and exited the cabin.

Treegar looked at Dr. Scordato. He was laying in his chair like he would rather it was a bed. "You and Dr. Nagi should take the bed upstairs. Garner and I will bunk down here, in case there is any trouble."

Scordato's nod was barely perceptible.

Concern needled Treegar. She pulled out her canteen and took a long pull from it. She put the cap back on before nudging Scordato's boot with her own. "You had anything to drink lately?"

"Hmm? Uh, no, I don't think so." He admitted groggily.

"Drink. Your body needs it. You're a doctor, you should know that."

"Right, yes. Thanks." He muttered and leaned down to his own bag and extracted his canteen. Just from watching him lift it, Treegar knew that he hadn't had a pull since they last stopped for food. What an idiot. Was he even listening to his body?

After he had drunk deeply from his bottle, he lowered it to his lap, leaving the cap off and not bothering to put it away.

Treegar sighed, "Look, we have a long way to go and we gotta look out for one another. But that also means that you gotta take care of yourself. We can't be dragging you along behind us. I know you're grieving, but the rest of us gotta know that you've got our backs. We need to be able to trust you to protect us, but how can we do that if we gotta remind you to drink and stuff? You get me?" She sank onto the arm of a squat settee and looked down at him as kindly as she could manage.

Dr. Scordato's shoulders could hardly slump any further but he nodded weakly.

Treegar looked around, eyeing the door that sat half-open and leaning against the side table. Then she reached up and flipped her visor up to give Dr. Scordato a clear view of her face. "Look, I know Agatha meant a lot to you. Losing her, it's gonna hurt for a long time. That pain, it isn't going anywhere. But you gotta snap out of this. There are things that have to get done. You want to bring her rings to her girls, fine, but if that's gonna happen then you've gotta do it. You die and those rings are as good as gone. The rest of us? We don't know her girls, don't have a clue where to find them, and I for one ain't gonna risk my neck bringing them a couple of keepsakes. You gotta live cause you have a mission that no one else can complete." She licked her lips, that was a lot more talking than she usually did, but it seemed to work.

Dr. Scordato looked more present and aware than he had since they left the base. He nodded and took another drink from his canteen. This time he put the cap on when he was done.

"They're in Vancouver. But you're right, I promised Agatha that I'd do this, you didn't."

Treegar nodded and stood up.

"Thanks." Scordato offered, looking up at her.

Treegar nodded sharply and turned toward the door.

A shadow flitted across the floor. Then it blots out the light.

Treegar flipped her visor back down and hastily glanced around for something useful to defend herself with. In an instant her blood is pumping and adrenaline surging.

Something pushes against the door. Treegar tenses.

"Hey, can you open this a bit more, I can't fit." Dr. Nagi's voice floats through the opening.

Treegar released a tense breath and lurched forward to drag the side table further from the door. Dr. Nagi steps through, her arms outstretched and laden with a small pile of sectioned logs. She carries them to the fireplace and drops them on the tiles. After a moment of swinging her arms and stretching her neck, she looks up at Treegar. "Thanks! Garner was right, there is a shed on the other side of the building, it's only about half full but it should be more than enough to warm this place up for a bit."

Treegar nodded and glanced back at the door, her adrenaline and anxiety hadn't abated despite the revelation that there was no real cause for concern.

"Relax, destroying the meteorite seems to have effected Xeno-1, there shouldn't be any infected to worry about" Dr. Nagi stated, stretching her arms a little bit more and then moving to the door.

"But if there are?"

Dr. Nagi frowned.

"Never count your chickens before they hatch." Treegar quoted.

"But we've been out here for days and haven't encountered any..."

"That's no reason to let your guard down." Garner countered, coming in with arms laden with firewood. "The infected aren't all we have to worry about out here. We need to start fashioning weapons." Nagi moved aside to let him pass. He brought his load to her pile and knelt to allow the logs to tumble carefully on top of hers.

"What?" Dr. Nagi started protesting.

"Jaspreet." Dr. Scordato interrupted, "Better safe than sorry. We don't know that it worked or even how what I observed in the lab will affect what we find out here."

Dr. Nagi pursed her lips and reluctantly nodded. "You're right, of course." She sighed, "I just hope…"

"We all do." Garner agreed, "but we can't count on hope when the price of being wrong is so high." He stood and put a hand on her arm, "I'll get the fire started, you show Treegar the woodshed and bring in some more."

"Right. Come on."

Treegar followed Dr. Nagi out of the cabin and back into the bright, snow-covered landscape. The sun dipped low on the horizon. It would be nice to stay behind something more solid than a tent for a night or two.

*   *   *

They stayed in the cabin for two nights. Jason and Jaspreet spent their time sleeping, eating, and huddling under blankets trying to recover a warmth Jason thought he might never feel again. The soldiers on the other hand, were busy scouring the building, the shed, and the surrounding forest for any and all potential weapons.

Jason hadn't noticed until Garner brought in an axe and placed it on the kitchen counter beside a collection of three small knives. From there a saw, the fire poker, and four walking sticks/spears were slowly added.

After their second night Jason found the soldiers strapping the knives, axe, and saw to themselves.

"Good morning! Breakfast is staying warm by the fire. Eat up and then it's time we got out of here. I trust you are feeling a bit better?"

"Um, yeah." Jason admitted. He was stiff and sore, but his legs felt better and Jaspreets injury hadn't leaked through the bandages overnight. His mind felt clearer than it had since this ordeal began, and fatigue wasn't lurking at the edges of his mind. All said, it was a lot better than when they had arrived.

The talking-to he had received from Treegar had helped clear a little of the fog while rest and food had done the remaining work. He was still mourning Agatha but that propelled him forward rather than anchoring him down. He would bring her daughters her rings. It was all he could do.

He picked up the bowl that had been left on the stones in front of the fire for him and drank the brothy contents, only using a spoon to force the final noodles and chicken chunks into his mouth. It took him only a minute or two but in that time the soldiers had finished gearing themselves up and were leaning impatiently beside the door.

Jaspreet walked out of the kitchen while twisting to double check her jacket closures.

"Put your bowl in the sink and grab your walking stick. Have you already packed your bag?" Garner asked.

"It's good to go, just upstairs," Jason lied and hurried past Jaspreet to leave his bowl beside hers. He then rushed up the stairs and hastily threw the last of his things into his pack and closed it up. When he rejoined the group by the door, Jaspreet held out a tall walking stick to him and he accepted it.

"Those are your best defense if we encounter anything. Treegar and I will try and take point whenever possible but if something comes at you, you stick it with the pointy end, got it?" Garner looked between the two doctors until they both nodded their heads emphatically.

"Good, we will be running drills with you as we go." He paused as though about to say something else and then shook his head, Jason felt vaguely cheated by that decision. "Double check your pack and then let's get going. We are losing daylight."

Jason swung his bag around and fumbled through its contents even though he had literally just thrown everything inside. Nothing in it felt personal outside of the few articles of clothing that had been pulled from his bunk and shoved inside. Everything else from the food to the bedroll were generic and impersonal in the extreme. The only really important things, Agatha's rings, were in the left side pocket and Jason fingered them with a mixed feeling of regret and comfort.

He closed the bag back up and gave Garner a nod. With that the group moved out into the cold and brilliant morning.

*   *   *

They stuck to the trees now. There were certainly areas where this wasn't an option but there weren't any more endless expanses of white nothingness. The trees grounded them. They also scared them. Snow fell from branches and sent them all scrambling to defend themselves. Wind shifted the branches and swayed the trunks causing scratching and creaking until the group had no hope of distinguishing animal movement from that of the trees.

For two days, between jumping at noises, Garner and Treegar drilled Jason and Jaspreet in their use of their spears. "Hit that bush." "Turn and strike that tree." "Quick behind you!" Over and over, till they could reliably jump and thrust at the drop of snow from a branch.

This meant that their nerves never took a rest. They walked on rubbery, aching legs, bracing themselves on tired arms but still ready to leap at the hint of a threat.

Unfortunately, threats seemed to be everywhere.

A drip. A creak. A heightening in the ever-present moan of wind through trees. Everything threatened. By the afternoon Jason was too exhausted to see straight.

SCREE!

The sound resounded from his left, sending him into a spin, nearly overbalancing into the soldier behind him. He thrust his spear forward into the air but instead of an empty threat he saw a squirrel. Grey and skeletal, its long tail matted and its eyes clouded over. A long quiet moan of pain escaped its slack jaw and it limped incautiously toward them.

Suddenly it stopped about a metre away, cocked its head to one side and then the other, twitching and sniffing the air. The moaning stopped. It backed up a step. Then another. It fell. The clouded eyes darted back and forth.

Then a spear point came crashing down on it, spilling the contents of its head into the snow.

Jason tore his gaze from the remains of the squirrel to the soldier who had ended it. Treegar yanked her spear up, the squirrel following it for about six inches before sliding off. She used the clean snow beside the squirrel to clean the tip of her spear, watching the squirrel for signs of further movement.

"Something's wrong." She commented, swinging her spear back into a walking stick position.

"You're telling me." Garner agreed.

"It was moaning." Jaspreet breathed; her gaze locked on the squirrel's remains.

"And it backed away from us."

"It was scared." Jason added, feeling the truth of the statement.

20

Cycles gained meaning once more. Darkness brought cold. It became harder to hunt but the pain grew less. Light brought warmth and a resurfacing of the pain and the search for food and lives. This was true throughout its expanse. Although the virus had noticed the dark and the light did not reach its parts at the same time. No, by the time the parts on the new land reached darkness, the ones in the warm land were nearly light again. This concept was all that rose above hunger and pain.

*　　*　　*

They moaned less at dawn. It was still the best time to go out, despite the slowly warming weather. Frost still bit the ground, gluing infected to it. Trapped in place, moaning their hunger and pain. It was a good warning system. You always knew when they were getting near, but they were more rapid than before and their noise triggered a primal fear within Charissa's gut.

The first days after The Change, and that was how Charissa was referring to it in her mind, were spent huddling in the deepest parts of the house, listening, absorbing the sound until it vibrated in their souls. When they ventured from that corner, they began by examining every inch of the interior of the house for cracks and weak points and then fortifying them as best they could. Attacks came with more than just relentless scratching now and several points which had been worn away over the past months nearly provided entrance to the infected.

It had been frightening to find so many weak points. That fear pushed Charissa and Timothy outside for their first supply run since The Change. Moving past frozen infected, they made their way to their neighbor's house and began dismantling it for parts. Cabinets, doors, siding, anything they could remove and transport were collected and relocated into their own home.

With all they could strip taken from the first neighbors home it was time to search another. Food was still an issue and while the worst of the weak points had been covered, Charissa at least wasn't comfortable with how little there was between where they slept and the monsters outside.

*   *   *

They crept up to the new house, skirting around frozen bodies. There is no sign of movement within and hasn't been for the three days they spent watching it before they decided to move. Charissa and Timothy creep up to the door and test the knob. It was, unsurprisingly, locked.

Timothy bent and picked up an ornamental frog, turned it over and pulled a key from its hiding spot. Charissa guessed that this was a benefit of raiding a neighbour's house.

The door opened and the pair slipped into the interior, pulling the door closed behind them. They entered a rec room with a large TV covering one wall and three different gaming consoles arranged under it. A small pool table stood next to a bar. Everything was layered in a fine film of dust.

Timothy moved deeper into the room. He placed his bag on the pool table, casting a puff of dust into the air. He motioned for Charissa to stand guard. She turned her back on him and scanned the space, alert not only for movement but also for any change in the ambient sound.

Bottles clinked behind her. She cast a quick look at what Timothy was packing up. Whiskey, bourbon, and beer. She looked away and back out into the still room.

"Let's keep going." He whispered. His bag was only half full and plenty of the alcohol remained on the shelves behind the bar.

Charissa shrugged, now was not the time for questions. They proceeded out of the rec room, past two closed doors and then stopped at a third. Timothy slowly turned the knob and eased the door open.

This room didn't have any windows so they were forced to turn on their flashlights. Charissa did so begrudgingly, it ruined her night vision and made them more visible to others. Still, doing so allowed her to see the treasure trove they had just found. Shelves covered in cans, boxes, and bags. All full of food. She clicked her jaw shut and got straight to work filling her bag.

It took only a few moments to fill her bag, barely denting the pantries supplies. Then she switched bags with Timothy and began wedging things between and on top of the bottles.

When it could barely zip up, she closed it and swung it on to her back. "Ready."

Charissa followed Timothy out the door, pulling it closed behind her. They turned off their flashlights and allowed their eyes to readjust before moving forward through the hall and into the rec room. The rising sun brought increased light into the yard. Charissa watched their surroundings while Timothy locked the door and pocketed the key.

In an instant they were swiftly moving around the house to their own door. Charissa again watched their surroundings while Timothy knocked.

Something moved across the street. A flicker in one of the windows. The pink house with the white trim, something moved. Charissa's arm hair rose and the back of her neck prickled. Something was there.

Penelope opened the door and the pair hurried inside.

"There's something in the pink house." Charissa reported while stripping off her gear.

"Are you sure?" Penelope said, her eyes widening and her voice pitching upward.

Charissa nodded, "I saw something move. It might be a person, it might not. We should steer clear of that one and maybe start entering through the back."

Timothy nodded. "Good idea. We should make another run tomorrow, get as much brought back here as we can."

"Speaking of, why the booze?" Charissa voiced her earlier thoughts.

"Medical supplies." Timothy responded succinctly.

"They are antiseptics and rudimentary pain relief." Penelope clarified. "Not for recreational use."

Charissa nodded, "Gotcha, don't worry about me raiding that stash, the thought of being anything less than sharp right now gives me the heebie jeebies."

*   *   *

The next few dawns see Charissa and Timothy emptying the neighbour's house. Slipping out the back door and returning with bags heavy with food.

Charissa kept an eye on the pink house, searching for further signs of movement. None were evident but that only increased her anxiety, the feeling of being watched never quite fading.

On the fifth day of watching she saw them. Not at the pink house where it continued to appear lifeless and empty, but at the end of the street. One by one, fresh unfrozen infected wandered past. Moaning, screaming, whimpering, and new.

Some were missing chunks of arm or leg. Others trailed their intestines. Some had bitemarks and segments of their faces missing. They wandered without purpose, hitting cars and houses and then adjusting course to continue on. Several approached their home, when they did Charissa pulled away from the window, replaced the shutter and then cowered behind it, listening to the moans and the sounds of them hitting the house.

She refused to breathe till her lungs felt like they would burst.

Slowly they stopped bumping into the house and she permitted herself to breath low shallow breaths. Her skin was covered in goosebumps and she was shaking, arms wrapped around her knees with the winter chill seeping through her layers of clothing.

On hands and knees, she eased herself away from the outer wall of the house and moved inward to their room, only standing right before she stepped inside. It took her a moment to adjust to the artificial light. Timothy had his arm around Penelope, Sophia and Atticus wedged in between them. Sophia held a book and sounded out the words while Atticus periodically flipped the pages.

"Not yet, go back." Penelope chided softly to her son.

Atticus flipped the page back and Sophia restarted the line that had been cut off.

"Not I said the duck."

"Okay, now." Penelope prompted and Atticus eagerly flipped the page.

Suddenly the scene shifted and Charissa could see them all covered in horrible wounds. Infected.

She stifled a gasp and blinked the image away. Tentatively she forced herself into the room and down onto the edge of the bed. Not part of the family circle, but close enough.

Penelope gave her a worried smile.

"Later." Charissa mouthed silently.

*   *   *

After the kids had fallen asleep, Charissa began to whisper what she saw to Penelope and Timothy.

"There are new infected out there."

"Oh." Timothy sounded less surprised and more disappointed.

"How new?" Penelope queried.

"A day or so? Maybe as much as a week."

Timothy and Penelope looked at each other. "I guess that's it then." Timothy said, "We hunker down again. Hope they pass us and hope we don't run out of anything important before we can make another run. Did any of them notice us? Attach themselves to the house?"

Charissa shook her head, "A few ran into the house but they moved on before I came to the room. I did my best to make sure they didn't see or hear me, but…" She shrugged and made a helpless gesture.

Penelope nodded and sucked her lower lip in between her teeth. "You did the best you could.

21

After the cycle came an awareness of space. Though all minds were one in it, the virus knew they were distant to each other. When the hunger and pain lessened enough, the virus calculated their space.

*   *   *

The engine sputtered out. Jason utilized the remaining momentum to eke out a few more metres before it slid to a reluctant stop. They'd reached the highway a few days ago, at least they were pretty sure it was the highway. It cut a clear, if snow-covered, path through the trees and mountains in a generally southern direction, with a smattering of abandoned cars along the route.

Jason could guess at what had happened to the vehicle's owners. What was surprising was Treegar's efficiency at hotwiring cars, a skill which she did not elaborate on.

This was their second vehicle, a red four-door Kia Rio hatchback, and until a moment ago it had been purring along and tackling the snow like a champion. The manual shifter allowed him to navigate the snow and ice with greater ease despite the occasional sliding and skidding. On the empty road, so long as they didn't roll, everything was fine. At least that's what he told himself, although there had been moments while coming down that last mountain that he had been pretty sure they were about to go over an edge and die.

But they made it. Jason sighed and gave up on wringing any further momentum from the little car. Treegar opened her door before anyone else, allowing a blast of cold air into the vehicle.

There was no use in arguing, Treegar would just glare at him, shrug and start walking away. Jason sometimes got the impression that she would be perfectly happy to just dump them all and make her way alone, which didn't exactly jive with some of her earlier behavior. Treegar didn't have to come, she had chosen to leave with them. Maybe she'd decided that she was wrong or maybe Jason was misinterpreting the enigmatic Corporal.

He much preferred Garner, or Vincent as he insisted on being called. He at least talked, answered questions with more than a shake of the head or a stern lecture. When they had reached the first of the bombed-out sections of road, Vincent explained what they were. Jason thought the road had just run out, that they weren't actually on a highway, that the snow had disguised a frozen river or something similar. Garner hadn't agreed and the further south they went the more evidence Jason saw that the soldier was correct. Vast sections of the road were pockmarked with craters. Every significant settlement they found had burnt out and abandoned buildings. Some had nearly been leveled completely.

Despite that, the increase in settlements meant two things: more supplies and more infected.

*   *   *

The house was too good to be true. Big, well stocked, a Silverado truck in the driveway. Treegar wasn't surprised when they found the remains of an infected human in the garage. It wasn't moving, for which she was grateful, but the stench clung to the inside of her helmet and made her stomach lurch. They made no attempt to move it, just locked the door and shoved a bookcase against it.

She shuddered; she didn't know what had infected that person or where it went after it had. She didn't say anything but kept her eyes open. It would be a bad idea to freak out the Doctors. They had been holding up well, even pulling their weight when they could.

They were getting almost good with their spears. Dr. Nagi had even taken down an infected rabbit the other day. Granted, the rabbit hadn't been moving very fast and had stopped dead when it got close to them, but the doctor had landed the fatal blow. The increase in confidence was clear in how her shoulders and stance shifted, both taller and straighter.

Guns were still an issue. Canada's gun control laws meant that most people either didn't have a gun or kept them in safes with the ammunition separate. This house had a safe which increased their total of found guns to three and provided them with a dozen more bullets. Treegar almost wished for the open gun laws of the United States, how nice would it be to happen upon a stash of guns with buckets of ammunition? But something like that would inevitably back fire in some way, either by setting a bunch of armed lunatics around or well… Treegar wasn't sure. Not that such wishful thinking was helpful right now.

At least tonight they had beds and tomorrow, transportation.

22

Understanding space led to a knowledge of what it had lost. It had once known things. Been aware of more than the rotting senses of its minds. Hunger and pain were distractions that had once not troubled it. They wore at it and the bodies it inhabited. Exhaustion drove too many of them down and it infuriated the virus to lose them.

*   *   *

Something about The Change compromised the infected's ability to sense prey. So long as they didn't catch Charissa watching their passage they simply walked past. Even those that caught a glimpse of her moved on after a few hours. But still, those hours did damage. The bolsters they had scavenged from the neighbour's home kept them out but several places in the siding were growing thin and would need to be replaced soon.

It had been two weeks since their last run, since she had seen the first of the new wave. A false spring kept them from freezing at night so they simply wandered unceasingly. Charissa wasn't even certain it would have stopped these new Infected. With their bodies so fresh would the mild west coast winter have affected them as it had their more decayed predecessors?

Charissa had begun to track them, writing short descriptions to designate them; pink sweater, tall guy, track pants, etc. She tracked not only how many she saw but what they looked like and if they returned, including times of arrival and departure. The numbers had grown until three days ago but since then they had dropped off again, many of the regulars missing from their usual rounds. There had been no gunshots and no obvious herdlike movement so Charissa could only assume they had begun to wander off or break down as the first wave had.

"I need to stretch my legs." She heard Timothy's voice rumble through the open door.

She couldn't make out Penelope's reply, only the lilting of her voice carried.

"I know it's dangerous… Numbers are going down… A few days from now… Ask her." His voice rose and dipped so Charissa only caught fragments, but she knew what this meant: he wanted to do another run.

Charissa looked out the currently empty street, could she go out there knowing what she knew? She wasn't sure that she could.

She didn't know how he could either.

But the question hadn't been put to her yet so worrying about it wouldn't get her anywhere, but the forewarning gave her the opportunity to plan. She would set a minimum number of acceptable Infected. Five, or maybe three, something low but not impossible. Something to put Timothy off for a little while but still give him something to look forward to.

The door opened behind her and she glanced back, it was Penelope.

"Hey."

"Hey."

"How's it looking out there?"

Charissa pretended to consult her notes, as though she didn't have their contents burned into her brain. "Six so far today. Eleven yesterday."

Penelope blew out a long breath, the air ruffling Charissa's loose hair. "So many."

"The number is dropping." She peeked back at the street, still empty.

"Yeah… still." Penelope trailed off and Charissa looked back at her. Her brow was creased and she had pulled her lower lip between her teeth.

Charissa waited to see if her sister would bring up her conversation with Timothy or not.

"What do you think is happening to them?" She finally asked.

Charissa shrugged, "Might be moving on to look elsewhere, might have been killed. I honestly don't know."

"Killed?"

"Maybe. I haven't seen anyone out there doing it, but it is possible. Wouldn't count on it though."

"But it's possible." It wasn't so much a question but rather an observation that Penelope was making to herself.

"Like I said, maybe. I haven't heard any gunshots, besides I'm pretty sure that would have drawn more of them in."

"But they could have used a knife or… or if they didn't want to risk getting too close, maybe a spear." Penelope's eyes widened and she almost smiled, "Oh, I have an idea."

Charissa furrowed her brow, checked the street again, and then returned her attention to her sister. "What?"

"Why don't we start killing them?"

"Huh?" Charissa pulled back and then asked, "What?"

"What if we created a kill zone? Here, or on another part of the house, somewhere they could see someone, get close, and then have us spear them without us needing to leave the house. We could cut down on their numbers with almost no risk to ourselves." She leaned forward looking more and more excited.

She looked insane to Charissa.

"Do you have any idea how hard it is to break a human skull?"

Penelope waved the question away. "About as hard as it is to smash a watermelon."

Charissa wasn't sure that that was true but had no real data to refute it with.

"No, see, if we can cut down on their numbers then they aren't out there Infecting more people. This is good… this might work. I'm going to go talk to Timothy about it." She flashed a smile at Charissa, "I'll be right back."

Charissa fidgeted with her notes, glancing between the numbers and the street. An infected was visible at the end of the road, number seven for today. It was a repeat from yesterday. A woman wearing a yellow rain coat a lot like the one Charissa had worn on her supply runs. She limped down the street moaning in quiet agony, the hood of her coat pulled back revealing clumps of dirty, matted hair. Her face was a mask of burns and oozing welts.

Charissa ducked away from the window and closed her eyes. The image of her trying to plunge a spear into the head of that woman flooded unbidden into her mind. She shoved it away, her stomach churning.

She drew in slow purposeful breaths until the image and the resulting queasiness faded and she dared to look out the window.

The woman stood in the middle of the street and stared at Charissa.

Charissa flinched back from the window and hid, her heart racing and the hairs on her arms standing on end.

*   *   *

"I'm just not comfortable with it." She admitted to Timothy and Penelope.

"Honestly, neither am I." Timothy confessed and then gave his wife a small nod of acknowledgement, "But what else can we do? Penelope's plan would work. We can't use guns; we only have so many bullets and the noise would just attract attention. This way we are at least fighting back."

Charissa took a measured breath, pushing her fear to the side and trying to look at the argument logically. "Fine, but I say we wait for a few more days. We need time to prepare; make spears and organize a kill zone. We should also fortify the walls in that area." As she began planning the fog of fear lifted and she was better able to focus.

Penelope nodded, "Right, well let's take a look at what we are working with."

Charissa glanced over at Sophia and Atticus, this whole situation was taking a toll on them. The once vibrant, active children were now quiet, slow moving, and exhibiting the same signs of prolonged fear that their parents were. It broke her heart. What kind of world was this to grow up in? What kind of adults would it produce?

Maybe that was what propelled Penelope and Timothy, the desire to somehow fix this situation for their kids. Rather than cowering in fear and hoping that someone out there would fix this, they were doing what little they could to make the world better. She imagined how a few short months ago they would have been all over her and their parents, asking questions and offering to help with various parts of the plan, eager to be included in the sacred world of adults. Now they preferred to lose themselves in their tv shows, too scared and worn down to reach out.

The adults planned for hours, reviewing their supplies and sorting them into groups, and choosing the best place for their plan.

"We need a funnel."

"But what if it gets clogged?"

"How do we make them go where we want them too?"

Thoughts and ideas were flung around, sketched out, and discarded.

"What about moving it around?"

When the sun set, they hadn't reached a consensus but the energy in the house had shifted. Even the wide, watchful eyes of the children reflected it. There was a wind of hope and purpose freshening up the stagnant air when they all gathered for bed.

However, when Charissa closed her eyes the faces of the infected haunted her dreams.

*　　*　　*

Charissa's lookout window became the default kill point. Mostly because no other room could be closed off from the rest of the house and had a good view of the street. It used to be the kids play room but it had been closed for weeks and was rarely used anymore.

The adults tried to keep the kids within their line of sight and, for their part, the kids tried to stick to their parents. Charissa listened to the soft chatter of Atticus and Sophia pretending to kill infected, fighting them to save princesses and kittens. She wondered if this horror would forever be a part of their play, if their innocence was gone forever.

Spears had been made from mop and broom handles. Knives were taped to their ends and tested to make sure that they were secure. When the street was empty, Timothy and Charissa placed unused furniture out on the lawn as obstacles to hopefully direct the movements of the infected. Interior and exterior walls had been covered in hastily scavenged siding, both neighbouring houses now showed large gaps where pieces had been pried off.

Today was the day they were testing their plan. Charissa shook with fear and anticipation, part of her wanted to flee while the other wanted an infected to show up so that it could begin.

They waited in cycles, two at a time, four-hour shifts. Hours ticked by with no infected.

Just after noon when Penelope switched places with Timothy one began wandering up the street. It lurched its way down the pavement with slow and ponderous steps coming closer and closer. Infection made its features bloated and puffy, the skin a putrid and rotting grey. The eyes looked like twin holes sunken into suffocating flesh.

Charissa gripped her makeshift spear and her hands slipped with sweat.

"Ready?" Penelope whispered.

Charissa nodded and hummed her ascent.

Penelope unlocked and swung open the window. "Hey!" She called out to the infected.

They turned and looked at the sisters, their mouth fell open and their moans grew into a scream. Their stride grew quicker and, in a moment, they were barreling toward the house.

Charissa and Penelope braced their spears in front of them and tensed. Charissa tried to keep her spear aimed toward the creature's head. She misjudged and her knife pierced their shoulder.

The scream became a howl as the infected pushed itself deeper on to her spear, forcing itself closer to its prey. Charissa felt frozen, bracing against it as it thrashed closer and closer.

The creature suddenly dropped, wrenching the spear handle from Charissa's grasp. She clung to it for a fraction of a second before it pulled her forward and into the window sill. She released the handle and stumbled backward.

Charissa gasped for breath and looked down at her red and aching hands and then up at Penelope. Penelope gave her a triumphant smile. "Grab a new one."

Charissa reached toward the pile of spears.

Penelope gasped and Charissa whirled to follow her gaze out the window. Two new infected were making their way hastily toward them, hunger and haste evident in their entire bodies. Charissa scrambled to get her new spear into position.

The first infected reached the fallen one and stumbled over it. Penelope took that moment to stab her spear into its skull. The knife slid deep into its brain, trapping the blade. When the blade refused to withdraw, Penelope used the spear shaft to push the infected into the path of its companion.

Charissa adjusted her grip and then plunged her spear forward and felt her knife slide through the hard shell of bone and into the infected's brain. The creature shuddered for a moment before dropping off of her blade and slumping into the pile of bodies.

Both women readied themselves for another wave of infected but when none came Charissa reached a trembling hand out to close the window. With a barrier between them and the world she turned to face Penelope, opening her mouth to say something. No words came out. Her tongue felt thick and her stomach heaved. With a split seconds warning she turned her head and the entire contents of her stomach exited through her mouth, splattering the wall and floor with chunks and bile.

Her body felt overly hot, covered in cold sweat as she retched again and again till nothing else would come up and her stomach ached from heaving. As her breathing returned to normal, she became aware of continued retching sounds. She turned her head and saw Penelope bent over her own pile of sickness.

Charissa used her spear and the wall to help her straighten up, Penelope moving only moments after her.

"That… went well." Penelope muttered, her face covered in a sheen of sweat and her eyes glassy.

"Yeah," Charissa sighed, "I'll go get some towels."

23

Furry drove the virus. It could not regain what it had lost but it was loath to lose more, to hunger, to decay, or to exhaustion. It would spread, it would gather all into itself and then, something inside of it knew, then it would be safe and whole.

*　　*　　*

He was done, just done. Done with living in his office. Done with stupid emails. Done with being responsible for this mess. Really, who wants to be responsible, even in part, of the apocalypse?

So yeah, he was done. He was sitting at his desk, staring at his computer screen at a list of reports waiting for him to read them, and he was done. He knew what those reports would say, it was the same everywhere. Xeno-1 was spreading.

With the infected now announcing their presence tracking them had become more accurate, but it just painted a dismal picture. It had reached the equator, shifting into warmer climates and infecting every bird, cat, or person it met. China and Japan had issued orders to kill all birds. So far there were confirmed infestations in North and South America and Asia. Uninfected countries had gone into the tightest lock downs possible, with several border countries killing anything approaching their borders on sight.

Greg wasn't certain how much of North America was left. Analysts told him that the human population was on a steady decline, currently sitting at a tenth of what it had been before Xeno-1 began its slaughter. Animal and avian populations though? They said they were likely extinct or nearly so.

The question of whether or not they could control this thing had been answered, they couldn't. It had rolled over them with the cold indifference of a tidal wave and all they could do was hunker down and hope it would pass them by.

And now it might be sentient.

Greg was done. He just wanted to go home. He wanted a decent cup of coffee. He wanted to curl up in his bed with his favourite book and listen to his favourite music and forget the past several months. But none of that was going to happen.

It wasn't just that his house was empty, abandoned and probably completely frozen. It wasn't just that the roads hadn't been plowed in who knows how long. It wasn't even that his car probably wouldn't be allowed out of the parking garage. No, it was that he was too smart to kill himself like that and he hated it.

With a sigh he forced his eyes to focus on the reports. Sentient. Great. Now morality would pop up again, never mind that it was mindlessly killing everything it could. It might be sentient so we are obligated to try and communicate with it. That was all well and good for the Aussies and the Europeans but it didn't really change things here in ground zero.

* * *

Treegar froze. The sound of a gun's safety clicking off ricocheting through her nerves.

"Turn around, nice and slow." A voice called out from behind. It was strong and authoritative, the voice of someone who had done this before. Not that that was a surprise, after all, they had managed to sneak up on her.

Treegar slowly turned her feet and moved her body around to face her hunter. There was a pair of them, standing on a short rise, staying atop the snow by virtue of wooden snowshoes. Their hunting rifles were raised and aimed at herself and Garner, though their fingers remained off of their triggers.

The taller of the two whistled and several more snowshoe clad hunters appeared around the group. Treegar looked around, five. She licked her lips and did some quick mental math. Maybe, if they all acted at once they could overwhelm these guys, but the odds of someone getting shot were high, very high. She dropped her spear and lifted her arms in surrender.

Garner and the doctors did the same.

"Smart. Hand over your weapons. You'll be coming with us." The original speaker ordered, Treegar assumed that made him the leader of this little hunting party.

She reluctantly swung her gun off of her back and unsheathed her various knives. Everything went into a pile beside her fallen spear. When she was almost out of weapons she pretended to be out, leaving a small boot knife tucked against her ankle.

Her arms again raised above her head, one of the hunters approached their group and began patting them each down, taking their bags and throwing them to the feet of one of their companions.

"That's everything?" The leader asked, the hunter nodded as did Treegar and company. "Good. Grab it and let's get back to base."

Three hunters, including the leader, held the group at gunpoint while the other two gathered up the guns, knives, and bags, stowing them together in large cloth duffel bags and then slinging them over their shoulders.

Once their stolen goods were packaged for transport, the hunters formed lines on either side of Treegar's group with one person taking up position behind them.

Treegar chafed at their easy capture, part of her wishing that she had made a move despite the high risk of herself or one of the others being shot. She watched her captors from the corner of her eye, analysing them for weaknesses and drawing comfort from the small knife rubbing rhythmically against her ankle.

*   *   *

The men were all wearing winter camo and equipped with what looked to Jason like high end hunting rifles. It looked like they had raided a Cabella's and made off with most of its inventory. They had a way of moving through the trees with practiced ease which made Jason feel like a lumbering oaf by comparison, it was no wonder they had managed to so easily sneak up on their group.

It only took about twenty minutes for the men to prod Jason and the others through the melting and dripping snow to a high wooden gate. It looked cobbled together from a variety of things, heavily improvised but sturdy. Like their outfits, the gate and the walls made Jason think that these people had stolen goods from all nearby stores. The one in the lead raised his fist high in the air and the gate began to swing open for them.

Jason gulped and took another frantic look around at his companions, at their captors, and at the open landscape. It took only that long for the gate to open far enough to permit one person entry and the hunters began herding their captives through the opening. Jason stared at the backs of Treegar and Vincent's heads, were they really not going to try and escape? Surely, they would signal and they would all break free in a moment.

But no, Jason's heart sank, they did nothing. Just like that they were all inside and the gate slammed closed behind them.

He looked up from his companions' heads to the awaiting courtyard. Dozens of sunken faced residents littered the space, grouped together in twos and threes. From among their number a tall man with a short grey beard smiled and strode up to the hunters and their prisoners.

"Welcome! My friends! Welcome!"

The lead hunter stepped up to the man, "Four bags of food, six guns and a bunch of knives."

"Gerald, my good friend, you missed the best part," The tall man looked past the hunter and Jason shivered at the hungry glint in the man's eyes, "You brought us interpreters."

The lead hunter nodded and reappraised his captives.

Jason felt his skin crawl and shook his head, as though the action would prevent whatever madness lay within these men.

The tall man stepped past the hunter, "I'm Wade, the leader of this community. I welcome you and the supplies you bring us."

Garner stepped forward, "That's nice and all, but we don't plan on staying. If you don't mind, we'd like to take our supplies and be on our way."

Wade spread his hands but sighed, "I'm afraid that is not possible. Come, let us discuss this in a more comfortable environment." He turned and motioned for the group to follow.

None of them moved. The tip of a gun pressed into Jason's back. "Get moving," a harsh voice whispered into his ear. The muzzle dug deeper and forced him to take a reluctant step forward, the rest of the group moving forward with him due to similar pressure.

He glanced back at the hunter prodding him. The man had a hard lined face with cold wide set eyes. Jason flinched away from the feral look the man gave him and took in the spectators. The people of this place had a thinness of recent hunger, it showed in the sallowness of their skin, the hollows of their cheeks, their sunken eyes. There was the same cold hunger in their faces as that of the hunter.

Jason shuddered to think what these people might be capable of. A little girl slid to the front of the crowd. She wore a muddy oversized coat and jeans so dirty Jason wasn't actually sure they were jeans. Her hair hung in clumps from under a loose red hat.

They were herded into a little white house. The floor in the entry way suggested that no one ever took their boots off and by the manners of the men leading and herding them this proved to be true. Jason was pretty sure he'd been in barns with cleaner floors.

Without the wind chill, Jason felt sweat break out along his lower back and under his arms. They were forced into a sitting room with several armchairs and a long sofa.

"Have a seat," Wade directed before sinking into an armchair. The hunters fanned out around the room, standing guard at the windows and exits.

Jason sat on the sofa and Jaspreet joined him. Garner and Treegar flanked them and chose armchairs that allowed them to watch most of their guards.

"I'm sure you have a lot of questions. We have a lot of questions too, like where are you from? And where were you headed? But before we get to answering any of those, how about we get a clear look at ya?" He motioned for them to remove their helmets.

None of them moved.

Wade sighed, "Come on." He waved at the guards who stepped forward menacingly and raised their guns a fraction.

Jason glanced at his companions. Garner gave a slight nod and they all began to comply, reaching up and lifting their helmets off their heads.

He felt exposed. Air brushed his shaggy, sweat matted hair and tickled his ears. Wade looked them all over as though they were prized horses. Jason wanted nothing more than to shove his helmet back on and get out of this creepy place with its overly cheerful wallpaper. From the look Wade was giving them Jason wasn't sure if the man was going to eat them or sleep with them and he honestly wanted no part of either scenario.

"Well now, isn't that better. I can see you and you can see me. How about we get to answering some of those questions, shall we?" Wade leaned forward, bracing his elbows on his knees and clasping his hands together while giving the group what Jason was sure he thought was a charming smile but under the circumstances came off false and smarmy.

The group silently stared back at him.

"Come now, I'm just dying to know. Where are you coming from? What's so important that you wanna leave here?"

Garner looked at the group and took a breath. "How about a trade? I answer one of yours and you answer one of mine?"

Wade laughed and leaned back into his chair with a satisfied smile, "Of course! Ask away! I want us all to be friends here."

"We are coming from a place just outside of Whitehorse. What is this place?"

"This," Wade gestured grandly, "Is Salvation!" He grinned at the group as though that answer meant anything. "Now, where are you heading that could be better than that?"

Jason cocked a skeptical brow but let Garner talk to this madman.

"We are trying to find some friends near Vancouver. What was this place called before?"

"Before?" Wade asked dismissively, "We were part of Lytton, but we are so much more than that now. We are the future. You don't want to go to Vancouver, there's nothing there anymore. Just a corpse being picked over by cowards. Here we have life! Here we have purpose!" His eyes lit up during his speech and his whole demeanor seemed poised on a knife's edge.

"Hmm," Garner undercut Wade's grandiosity, "I have more

questions."

Wade deflated a little but nodded permissively, "Of course, ask away."

"What did you mean by 'interpreters'?"

Wade smiled as though Garner had asked him about his favourite subject in the whole world. "How connected are you?"

That rejoinder threw Garner off, "To the internet? We aren't." His eyes shifted from Wade to the various members of his group. For the first time in the conversation betraying his confusion.

"Well," Launched Wade, "the lead scientists in this whole thing are saying that Xeno-1 is intelligent, or that there is some kind of higher form of intelligence controlling it." He pointed to the ceiling, "alien intelligence."

Jason's mouth fell open. How in the world had the man come to such a conclusion? Surely none of his or Dr. Nagi's speculations had been published openly. The man might not be entirely incorrect but... Jason did not have a good feeling about his conclusions.

"What does that have to do with us?"

"Well, you see, you look like smart individuals to me. All the infected we have out here are animals, birds and rabbits and such. You can't talk to a rabbit and expect sense."

Horror washed over Jason and he surged to his feet. "No! Absolutely not! That's insane!"

His companions stood as well, understanding washing over them in a slower but equally horrifying manner. Treegar and Garner braced themselves for a fight and the guards raised their guns and took aim.

"Now, now, no need to over react. Settle on down." Wade made wafting settling motions with his hands but didn't stand. "Is that anyway to thank us for our hospitality?"

Jaspreet scoffed.

Wade cast her a dismissive glance and then returned his gaze to Garner, "sit back down so we can discuss this like reasonable people."

When they made no moves to follow his directive, Wade shrugged, "Fine. You're right. We plan on infecting you. One by one mind, until we can talk to Xeno-1. I know that might not sound great to you but hey, look at it this way, you'll be part of science, part of something bigger than yourselves. You'll do something no one has ever done before. You'll go down in history as having saved humanity. What could be more noble?"

Jason remembered what it had felt like to deliberately give himself radiation therapy to better study Xeno-1. He thought of Jaspreet and all that she had left to come and study the meteorite. He considered how Agatha had died. He clenched his fists, this piece of scum in front of him didn't know a single thing about sacrificing for science. He just wanted guinea pigs. Disposable humans. Jason spat at the ground in front of Wade.

"I refuse to be your guinea pig. You don't know the first thing about what you're talking about."

Wade laughed. He actually laughed at Jason's anger and contempt. "Oh! And I suppose you do?"

"I do, in fact. I'm Dr. Jason Scordato, virologist. I know more about Xeno-1 than you could ever hope to." He snapped, this tone dripping with contempt.

Wade looked taken aback for all of two seconds before he slapped the arm of his chair and laughed again, "Well *doctor*, I guess you just volunteered to be first in line. I was going to go with your lady friend here," he pointed at Jaspreet, "but you'll do nicely. As a scientist and all, I wouldn't dream of depriving you of an up close and personal experience with what you claim to be studying." He barked another laugh and waved at the guards.

The guards moved in, one of them prodding Jason with the muzzle of their rifle again. Jason lashed out in animalistic instinct. He threw the hardest punch he could muster at the nearest man's face. His hand erupted into fiery pain as though he had hit a brick wall and the guard reeled back, stumbling into another guard.

Garner and Treegar moved a split second after him, wailing much more effectively on the guards nearest them. Jaspreet reached out and grasped a lamp off a side table and swung it at another guard.

Jason kicked and punched indiscriminately. The group worked their way through the guards and towards the door.

Jaspreet screamed as a guard wrapped their arms around her and dragged her away from the group. Jason snatched at her arms and wrenched her toward him, sending them both stumbling backward into the wall.

A gunshot went off.

Everyone froze.

"Now, now, none of that. You are all going to be quiet or we aren't even going to keep you alive long enough for our little experiment." Wade's voice barely penetrated the fuzzy echoing left in the wake of the gunshot. He stood in front of his chair holding a still smoking rifle, now aimed intently on the four of them.

The guards scrambled around them, readying their own guns.

"You go on now. No more funny business." Wade admonished in an aggravatingly paternalistic tone.

24

Fear. It was nearly always one of the last emotions felt before the virus joined a life. It was strange that the virus feared so little itself. Only fire, cold, and death had inspired fear for so long that it took the virus a long time to recognize a new one. It now feared losing control.

*   *   *

The kill box had its flaws but in the following days they learned to make those flaws work for them. Spears stuck or can't be pulled out without drawing the infected closer to you? Fine, drop the spear and grab a new one. When the coast is clear, use the stuck spear to drag the body away from the kill zone and then recover it. Infected getting too close? Insert spikes a few feet from the window, it either catches them or slows them down at the right moment. Scared? Use that to hit them harder.

It was working, or at least it seemed to. Four days and a dozen Infected neutralized. They were piling the bodies inside the second neighbour's rec room. It looked like the scene of a massacre and Charissa didn't want to think of the smell come summer time.

Luckily there didn't seem to be any small creatures among the second wave. Mostly people, one dog. That had been hard.

Charissa watched the street for her third hour. There had been no movement all day. That was a good sign, it meant they were making a difference. After the first day, she tried to focus on that, pushing thoughts of who these people were before they were infected with Xeno-1 out of her mind and focusing on the future.

It was easier if they were older, not in years but in terms of being infected. She didn't have an exact timeline, but you could tell. The longer they had been infected the thinner and conversely more bloated they became. Their muscles and skin sagged while gasses built up inside of them and made them bulge in strange ways. There was a spectrum, no two infected ever exactly the same. But it was easier when they didn't *look* human anymore.

An old one made its way down the street, stumbling on rotting legs. Even from several house lengths away she could tell that it didn't really look human anymore. Its eyes bulged over sunken cheeks, jaw jutting forward to reveal broken and yellowed teeth, the marks where it had been attacked obscured in the general discolouration and decay.

Charissa opened the window and readied her spear. It took only a brief second for the infected to register the movement and react. Unlike fresher bodies this one was unable to charge her, settling instead for a ground eating limp, its head thrusting forward and snapping its jaw.

It mindlessly threw itself onto a spike, lunging toward her with its arms and teeth. She plunged her spear between its eyes, burying the knife to the hilt and forcing its head back. It shuddered for a moment before dropping like a marionette with the strings cut.

Charissa drew another spear from the pile beside her and nodded at the waiting Timothy. One more hour and then her shift was over and Penelope would join her husband. She drew the window closed and sat back down, picking up a pen and adjusting their kill count to read 13.

*   *   *

"All clear!" Penelope called out.

Charissa opened the door and both she and Timothy slipped out.

Timothy closed the door behind them and the pair followed the familiar path through the kill zone. Their modifications made their house stand out in the street in a way that Charissa knew declared their location to any humans who might see. These efforts to lower the infected population also put a target on their own backs. She eyed the surrounding houses, particularly the pink one across the street for any sign of movement.

Working together they freed infected bodies from the spikes, utilizing embedded spears to leaver them and pull them out of the way. Timothy carried a spare spear which he wedged in where he could to assist in the removal. Once the bodies were clear of the spikes, Charissa grabbed the embedded spear and Timothy stabbed the body with his own, together they began dragging the corpse away from the house and down the slick path to the neighbours.

It was a familiar routine perfected over the past several days but that did not make it easy. After months of idleness, the removal of a single body took upwards of twenty minutes and left them both covered in sweat. Charissa's arms felt like wet noodles and it took pitting her entire weight against that of the corpse, with Timothy's help, to get the thing where they wanted to take it.

Halfway down the path Timothy stopped, "Did you hear that?"

Charissa's nerves sprang to life and she strained to hear what Timothy had heard. Only the distant ever-present moan of infected filled the air, like white noise drowning out the silence.

Thud

Charissa jumped and wrenched the spear out of the corpse. She met Timothy's eyes and they abandoned their work to move with quick but quiet steps back toward their house.

The front door was open. The gaping maw gave the house the look of a shocked face which Charissa could feel reflected in her own. She broke out into a sprint. Timothy's longer legs propelled him through the opening a moment before her. Charissa paused only long enough to assess the interior.

A scream tore through the house.

Charissa moved without thinking, sprinting up the stairs two at a time. Timothy raced ahead of her down the hall toward the bedroom.

A figure loomed out from the kitchen. Charissa plunged her spear into it, the tip glancing off something and she lunged in a second attack. The figure turned and dodged. The knife caught their arm and they cried out in pain.

Charissa stepped back in surprise, eyeing the intruder suspiciously. They clutched their arm and stared at her, a gun hanging from their injured side.

"You're alive." Charissa observed.

"So are you. If you want to stay that way, I suggest you step back and let us finish what we came here for." He spoke with confidence despite the blood now dripping on the tiled floor.

"Which is?"

"Supply run."

Charissa almost laughed, "You think I'm going to just step back and let you take our supplies?"

The man shrugged, "Either that or you die. It's your choice."

Charissa lunged, catching him unprepared in the throat with her spear. He gurgled for a moment, his eyes bulging. She ripped her spear back and a spray of blood hit the welding mask. The intruder fell forward and convulsed.

She looked around but didn't see any movement nor any signs that the man had companions in the hall. She knelt down and picked up his gun, checked that the safety was on and traded it for her bloody spear. There were voices coming from down the hall.

"Don't come any closer." A strange voice drifted from the open bedroom door. Charissa crept down the hall, careful not to make a sound.

"Look, whatever you want, take it. Just let her go." Timothy offered. Charissa watched from behind as he set his spear down in front of him and took a half step forward.

"I said stay back!" The man snapped.

"Okay, okay. "What do you want?" Timothy held his hands up in surrender.

"Get in the corner!" The man yelled.

Timothy nodded his head, "Alright. I'm going." He took slow exaggerated steps away from the door and Charissa melted backward further into the hallway's shadows.

With Timothy out of the way she could see a man in cobbled together plastic gear holding Sophia with his forearm around her neck and a gun held out in front of him. The little girl's brown eyes were wide and her face drained of her natural colour.

Charissa's heart stuttered at the sight and a cold fury swept over her. Slowly, while the man's eyes were locked on Timothy, she lifted the stolen gun and took aim. Time slowed. She felt like she could count her own heart beats. The man blinked. She squeezed the trigger and exhaled.

The man's head exploded, spraying the wall behind him with blood and ichor. Sophia dropped from his grasp and stumbled onto the floor. Only when she was free did Charissa's focus expand to the rest of the room. Her ears were ringing from the gunshot but even through that she could hear the screaming. So much screaming.

Penelope had Atticus tucked behind her in the corner furthest from the man's body. Both of them had visible tear tracks running down their faces. Their mouths were open and it took Charissa a moment to put together that they were the sources of the screams.

Sophia was crying and crawling toward her family. Timothy stood frozen halfway down the wall, his gaze turned to Charissa for a moment and then he swooped forward and reached for Sophia, only pulling back when he realized he was still wearing his outside gear.

"It's okay Sophie, you're okay." He began chanting, pulling his hand back and lifting the visor to unobscured his face. He dropped to his knees, his voice getting softer. And then he fell over.

"Daddy? Daddy!" Sophia yelled, reaching out and touching his jacket.

Charissa leapt forward, "Don't touch him!" She gasped.

Sophia flinched and snatched her hand back.

Charissa knelt down and began unbuttoning and removing what she could of Timothy's clothing. Her hearing was returning, though a high-pitched ringing remained. As she pulled open his rain jacket, she saw a growing stain of crimson on the front of his sweater. She gasped and reached out to place pressure on the wound.

"Tim!" Penelope leapt forward and interposed herself between Charissa and Timothy.

She reached out and placed her hands on the wound for a moment before retracting and staring at the blood on her palms.

"Help me remove his clothing." Charissa directed, moving around her sister to get a better view. The sound of her voice seemed to snap Penelope out of her momentary trance and she used her fingers to reach inside the blood-soaked entrance hole and grasp the sweater fabric. With a swift tug the material tore allowing better access to the layer's underneath.

Charissa followed Penelope's example by reaching in and tearing open the next layer. Penelope tore the next and Charissa ripped the last layer. Finally, the wound was laid bare, dark blood welling up from a ragged hole.

"We need to put pressure on the wound."

"Yes. Pressure, right." Penelope reached out and pressed her hands on the hole, blood squishing out between her fingers.

Timothy groaned and then a wet cough tore through his body, causing him to convulse against Penelope's weight. His eyes fluttered open but stared unseeing at the world above him.

"I'm going to get some towels. And the first aid kit. I'll be right back." Charissa said, jumping to her feet. "Keep the pressure on it. I'll... I'll be right back." Her gaze lifted from how Timothy's blood was rapidly spreading over Penelope's hands to the blood drained faces of the children. She spun on her heel and fled the room.

Towels. Pressure. Bandages. The words circled in her mind, carrying her to the bathroom. She swept as many towels off the shelf as she could carry and grabbed the first aid kit.

She returned to the bedroom and immediately dropped to Timothy's side.

He was whispering to his wife and kids, comforting them. "It's okay. I'll be okay." Okay, okay, okay. Over and over again till the word became a breath. Charissa focused on the word, she would make it okay.

She lifted Penelope's hands just long enough to slide a clean towel underneath. Penelope almost slammed her hands back down, her fingers leaving a halo of blood on the towel as they sunk in the sudden return of pressure making Timothy groan in pain even as he gritted his teeth to keep the sound inside.

Charissa unzipped the first aid kit, opening it and laying it on the floor. She dug through its contents reading labels and frantically wondering what she was doing. There were scissors, she pulled them out and began cutting away the remainder of Timothy's clothing. It fell away leaving his skin exposed to the cool air.

Now what?

She returned to the first aid kit and pulled out a sterile abdominal pad. Okay. She dug out some wipes. Clean the wound, bandage the wound. Oh Lord, what came after that? There were no hospitals to take him to. What had the bullet hit? What further complications would he have? Her mind spun in a million directions and her hands shook as she ripped open a wipe.

"Lift your hands." She directed Penelope who reluctantly complied.

Timothy's voice trailed off as fresh blood began oozing out of the wound. Charissa hastily wiped the area and tore open the abdominal pad, the tremors in her hands almost causing her to drop the pad on the floor. She placed it over the hole. The cotton white pad immediately soaking up the blood, soaking through the absorbent layers in moments. Charissa took another towel off of the pile and set it on top. She pressed into the towel.

"What now?" Penelope asked, her eyes on her husband's face where his lips kept moving in a silent chant but her words directed at Charissa.

"I don't know." Charissa admitted. "He needs a hospital, a doctor."

Penelope nodded; she already knew that. "Tim, Tim, Timothy." She gulped in the air. "Kids come here." She directed, drawing her children into her arms, the blood on her hands staining their shoulders.

Charissa pressed hard on the towel, feeling the fabric grow

damp.

"It's okay, It's okay." Timothy's voice was audible for a moment and then faded back to nothing. He let out a sigh and then stilled, his face drooping as the muscles relaxed.

Penelope let out a loud sob and both children turned their faces into her chest. Charissa lifted her hands, the blood has soaked through the abdominal pad and the towel to leave a pink staining on her skin. She blinked at it and then up at Penelope. Her sister and her children made a heartbreaking tableau of grief.

Charissa stood, their sobs rushing around her ears in white noise. The man who threatened them was still lying where he had fallen. The back of his skull adorned the wall, night table, and part of the bed. It was gruesome and definitely not something her niece and nephew needed to remember.

As though in a trance, she bent down and grabbed his limp arm. With all of her strength she began pulling. Slowly the body began to shift and drag behind her. Step by step she drew it out of the room and down the hall. A trail of blood and urine behind them.

"Stay where you are!" A familiar voice ordered.

Charissa froze.

"Stand up."

She dropped the man's arm and straightened. She berated herself for leaving the gun in the room. Out of the corner of her eye she could just make out this intruders' shadowy form.

"Turn around."

She took small steps to slowly rotate to face her new opponent. He was tall and familiar. "Ryosuke?" She breathed.

"What did you do to him?" Ryosuke demanded his rifle firm

against his shoulder and trained on her.

"I shot him." Charissa admitted, "He was threatening my niece."

"Your what?" Ryosuke gasped.

"My niece. She's six, almost seven. He… he threatened her." She couldn't work her tongue around the horror of that moment.

"There's a kid in here?" He asked incredulously.

"Two." Charissa admitted.

Ryosuke swore.

Charissa flinched.

"Get back in that room and close the door. Don't come out. Don't let anyone out." He directed, gesturing with the muzzle of his gun.

Charissa nodded. She took a careful step backward stepping between the tangled limbs of the man she had killed and went back into the bedroom. Penelope had arranged Timothy's hands on his chest and pulled his torn shirt over part of the towel. If not for the rent in his clothing and the pallor of his skin, he might have been sleeping.

Charissa picked up her discarded gun. She closed the door behind her with a click then pressed her ear against it to listen for Ryosuke's retreat. There was a faint creak from down the hall. She turned to look at Penelope and the kids again.

"There's more out there. They want us to stay here."

Penelope shook her head in a slow side to side swing. "We can't. They'll take everything."

"I know." Charissa acknowledged.

Penelope glanced at Timothy and then the children still curled into her. Slowly she uncurled the children from her side. "I need to help your Auntie, stay with your dad for a minute. I'll be right back." She said in a calming tone.

"No," Charissa said, "You should stay with the kids." She leaned down and picked up her dropped spear and held it out to Penelope. "Use this if you have to."

"I'm coming." Penelope said in a tone that brokered no argument but took the spear and used it to leverage herself off of the floor.

Charissa sighed and picked up Timothy's spear.

Penelope bent down and recovered the gun that shot her husband. "Let's go." With a final glance at her children and her dead husband, Penelope rolled her shoulders and gave Charissa a grim nod.

Charissa eased the door open without a single sound. The hall was empty except for the bodies of those she had killed. Ryosuke was gone.

She crept forward, sensing Penelope slip behind her. Together they moved to the end of the hall and proceeded down the stairs.

There were muffled voices coming up from the basement, rustling sounds, a thud. Charissa continued to the basement stairs avoiding the creaks through months of experience.

"Children! We can't just let them starve!"

"Who cares? This is about survival; they couldn't defend it so they don't deserve it!"

"That's disgusting! What about the future?"

"What about it? Seems like we have one and they don't. Survival of the fittest. Now get your head on straight and start carrying. Those gunshots are going to attract the Undead. I want most of this stuff moved before they get here."

Charissa was far enough down the stairs to see the two invaders. She crouched and took aim. Penelope eased in beside her and aimed her gun as well.

"Hey!" Someone at the top of the stairs yelled.

Charissa didn't spare them a glance and took her shot. The man talking to Ryosuke went down. She didn't think she had hit his head but she knew that she had hit something. She looked up at the top of the stairs where a woman gaped at her.

Penelope took her shot. The woman at the top of the stairs began barrelling toward them. Charissa braced Timothy's spear on the step below her and angled it into the woman's path.

The woman saw it and tried to side step out of the way but it was too late, her momentum carried her into the spear and she tumbled down the rest of the stairs, her hands sliding on the plastic of Charissa's rain jacket as she tried to pull her with her. She turned as she fell, the spear jutting out of her chest. Her eyes were wide, her mouth popped open air mixing with blood in a gurgling sound.

Charissa and Penelope followed her down to the basement floor. And looked around.

Both Ryosuke and his companion were down but neither was dead. Ryosuke clutched his stomach with one hand while grasping for his fallen gun with the other. His companion dragged unmoving legs to reach that same gun.

Charissa raised her gun again, controlling her breathing and letting her vision pinpoint again. "Who said we couldn't defend it?" She asked before squeezing the trigger and putting another bullet into him.

25

The pain and hunger became a part of it. Slowly the virus began to wield control over its selves rather than allowing their hunger and pain to control it. It was not a perfect process, hunger often won out.

*   *   *

The guards deposited them in a windowless room just off of the kitchen with marks on the walls where shelves had been removed. Treegar's best guess was that this had been a walk-in pantry, which probably put them more or less in the middle of the building.

The room had one light fixed to the ceiling, one door, and a whole lot of nothing else. Not even a blanket for the four of them to share. Wade certainly wasn't treating them like long term guests.

Which implied that he didn't expect them, any of them, to survive long. They would probably move forward on their insane plan within the next few hours. Maybe even sooner.

"We have to get out of here." Dr. Scordato's voice mirrored her thoughts.

Treegar started tapping the walls, listening to the sound they made. They were all made of painted drywall, which should make getting through them fairly easy, the tricky thing was figuring out what was on the other side. If they were very, very lucky they could make a hole into an unused room and escape through there. If they weren't lucky, they would punch a hole right in front of a guard.

"What are you doing?" Dr. Nagi whispered.

"Listening for hollow spots. I'm going to try and cut a hole." She nodded at the door. "They will be guarding the door because they expect us to try and escape through it. Actually, it wouldn't be a bad idea to try that, at least as a distraction. If you pound on it and yell a little, that should cover any noise I make."

"What?" Dr. Scordato gaped.

Treegar sighed and repeated herself. "Go, pound on the door, demand to be let out. Say whatever you want. Insult their mothers. I do not care, just make enough noise that they won't hear what I'm doing. If we are very, very lucky, then this just might work."

"And if we aren't?" Dr. Nagi's voice quivered.

Treegar shrugged, "Well, it won't be worse than what they have planned for us."

The doctor swallowed and nodded before flinging herself at the door and trying to force the handle open. When that failed, she began banging her fists against it and screaming.

"Hey! Hey! Let us out of here! You can't do this! It's murder! You're murderers! Let us out!" She went on and on, vacillating between terrified inarticulate pleas and loudly citing human rights and the Geneva Convention.

Treegar turned and put her ear back against the wall. Dr. Nagi's yelling and pounding interfered a little with finding a hollow spot but since the plan was mostly dependent on luck, it didn't really matter.

She pulled her knife from her boot, chose a spot and stabbed.

"What's that?" Dr. Scordato whispered.

Garner shushed him.

Treegar saw the doctor shake his head but he quieted down.

With the knife in the drywall she began to swing back and forth, first making a line, then when she hit a support, pulling the knife out and making a line along that support. She worked a rectangular piece out of the wall before someone banged on the door and screamed at them to shut up.

Dr. Nagi backed away from the door and looked fearfully at Treegar.

"It's okay." Treegar murmured, carefully keeping her voice just barely above a breath. "Talk to each other. Make plans. Ridiculous things, things that might throw them off."

Everyone nodded.

Garner cleared his throat and, in a tone just above a whisper, barely loud enough to carry, he declared, "It's no use, we just have to break down the door!"

Treegar shook her head at him and went back to her task. She stabbed the knife through the second layer of drywall and began cutting a matching rectangle out of it. The knife was dulling so this took longer. About the time the group had settled on tactics, she was through. She eased the rectangle out of the wall and pulled it through, into the pantry.

The hole was just big enough for her to put her head through so that is exactly what she did. The hole opened into a small bedroom with a double bed and a dresser. What she could see of it was devoid of art and, more importantly, of guards.

It was their best-case scenario.

She pulled her head back into the pantry and looked at her companions. The hole she had made wouldn't fit a person but she could break pieces off from it to make the hole bigger. She mimed this to Garner while they continued their mock debate.

Garner nodded, "Okay, I'm going to do it! Get into positions!" He approached the door, looked at Treegar, his expression one of hopeful determination, and then began throwing his weight against the door.

As his shoulder hit, Treegar ripped a chunk of drywall out, the two sounds melding into one. He did it again and she broke another chunk. And again. The hole on this side was big enough for her to reach though to the other side. She began widening that end.

When she could slide into the other room, she signaled for him to stop.

"Ow!" He yelled in a believable facsimile of pain, "I can't do it. I think I hurt my shoulder."

"Oh no!" Dr. Nagi gasped, "What can we do now?"

"We'll have to wait till they open it and then rush them!" Dr. Scordato asserted, "You did your best; we should all rest now so we will be ready when the time comes."

Treegar helped them all through the gap and then pushed pillows and blankets through the gap, awkwardly arranging them into humanoid shapes. She pulled the last pillow slightly into the hole behind her, hoping that it concealed the hole for at least a moment.

"Move over." Garner whispered.

Treegar rocked back on her heels and looked behind her. Garner and Dr. Scordato were holding the dresser between them. She half rolled-half crab walked out of their path and they carefully placed the dresser over this side of the hole.

"We need to find our gear." Treegar whispered.

There was no way they were leaving this place without their protective gear, if they wanted to die then they might as well have stayed in that room. The guards had taken their jackets before shoving them into the pantry and their helmets had been left in the sitting room. She had no idea where their bags might be. Best to focus on finding their main gear and just get out of here.

"You two stay here." She whispered to the doctors. "If we aren't back in ten minutes, climb out that window and get out of here." She slipped off her boot and wrinkled her nose at the odor her feet emitted. As noxious as it was and as dirty as the hallway floors were, it would be less of a tell than the sound of her boots.

Garner cocked a brow at her but joined her in removing his boots, the pungent odor of his feet mingling unsettlingly with her own. "Let's go."

She slid to the door and eased the knob around until the latch gave and she was able to soundlessly crack the door open. There was one guard in the hall with their back turned to the bedroom door. Treegar glanced down the other end of the hall before sliding out of the door.

With long, low sliding steps she eased in behind him, gripped her knife with her right hand and grabbed his head with her left, driving the base of his skull on to her blade. The palm of her left hand covered his mouth, smothering his dying sounds. His body dropped and Treegar sagged to keep him from pulling them both down. Blood and spinal fluid dripped down her hand, making the grip of her knife both sticky and slick. He convulsed and then the damage her small blade had done to his brain was complete and he was gone.

Garner was there in an instant, picking up the guards legs. The two carried the dead man into the room. They dropped him on the side of the bed furthest from the door. Treegar wrenched her boot knife from the man's skull and used his shirt to clean the fluids off of it and her hand.

When she looked up, the doctors were looking at her with horror. Treegar shifted her glance away from them and looked at Garner. His face was blessedly neutral.

Together they crept back into the hall. Treegar checked around the corner, she could see the front door and the open entrance to the sitting room. Two guards chatted in the foyer, relaxed and confident.

Treegar looked at Garner and as one they pulled back a half-step around the corner.

"We have to separate them." He signaled.

Treegar nodded. They retreated to the bedroom. When they eased the door back open, the doctors jumped into defensive positions before relaxing.

"There are two guards between us and the door. If we separate them, we have a chance at taking them both out." Garner informed them.

"How are we going to do that?" Dr. Nagi asked, glancing between Garner and Treegar. She was leaning forward on the balls of her feet, ready and willing to join in fighting for their freedom but her face still flinched when her eyes landed on Treegar.

"We need to draw one of them down the hallway. That's our best chance."

"I'm going to make a little noise, hopefully one of them comes to investigate." Treegar supplied.

"Wait, what about the other end of the hall? Did you check there?" Dr. Scordato asked.

Treegar shook her head, they hadn't checked.

"What happens if someone comes from over there? You'd be caught between. We all would be!"

She nodded, "You're right, I'll try to ensure that they don't hear it."

The doctor didn't look reassured but clamped his mouth shut.

Treegar turned back to the door and opened it for a third time. The hall was still deserted. Saying a silent prayer to Garner's God, and hoping that he was praying too, she closed the door again but allowed the latch to click loudly into place. She pressed her ear against the wood, straining to hear past the pounding rhythm of her pulse to hear if anyone reacted to her bait.

Nothing. Perhaps the sound had been too small? She didn't want to throw something out there for them to find. The risk of getting trapped between two sets of guards was too real for anything so reckless.

She eased the door open again and assessed the hall. At that moment a guard rounded the corner. Treegar held her breath and ducked back.

Too late.

"Hey!" He shouted and lunged after her.

Treegar sprang forward, knife first, ramming it into his throat. The blade slid across his skin, tearing a jagged line before hitting bone and glancing off. The slice instantly filled with deep red blood. The guard gurgled and fell into her. She braced herself and allowed him to make a controlled fall into the room. The spray of fluids soaking into her clothing and making it stick to her skin.

Garner helped her drag him the rest of the way in and then closed the door again.

The guard still grasped and gurgled as life flowed out of him and puddled on the floor.

Treegar had to look away. Seeing him suffer. Seeing how the doctors looked at her. Feeling his rapidly cooling blood on her skin. It made her feel ugly, empty and wrong.

She knew she wasn't doing it because she liked it. She knew she had no other choice. She knew that it was a matter of her life or theirs. Not just her life, the lives of Garner and the doctors, no matter that they judged her for it. She was doing this for them.

Treegar felt her shame morph into anger and indignation. It was better, more energizing. It masked the ugliness inside of her.

There was a voice in the hall. Then a shout and someone was at the door. They forced it open and sprang into the room. Treegar adjusted her grip on her knife and jumped the guard. He stood momentarily stunned by the sight of his friend bleeding out.

She went for his eye, the soft organ allowing her dulling blade entry. The side scraped his occipital bone, the sound grating in the stunned room. She pulled the knife out and let him fall on his friend.

Boots filled the hall. Three guards replaced the one who fell. They stared at her with open horror and malice. Treegar braced herself, imposing herself between the rest of the group and the guards. Her small knife raised to strike.

"What's going on here!" Wade's voice demanded. The guard's attention split toward the entrance way.

Treegar didn't hesitate. Her red stained blade flashed and bit into the throat of the nearest guard. She hit an artery, sending a burst of blood into her face.

That pulled the guard's attention back to her. Her victim clutched his throat, dropping his weapon to do so. Blood dripped between his fingers and he swayed back into his companions.

Wade cursed.

Treegar swept forward again, this time swinging low to reach for her victim's weapon. She grasped at the gun and tossed it behind her to her companions. There was a thud and the sound of fumbling. She was too busy keeping her eyes on the men before her to check if Garner or one of the scientists had the gun.

She watched the guards and they watched her. They had their guns up, ready to shoot but inexplicably holding back.

"Seems the prisoners are attempting to escape." One of the guards said.

"Well, stop them!" Wade yelled.

"Copy that."

The guards stepped into the room.

Treegar stepped back, watching warily for any sign of weakness. There were only two of them. Not great odds but her little boot knife had already taken out four of their companions, if she could get past their guns, she might stand a chance.

She swallowed, the metallic taste of blood clinging to her tongue and turning her stomach. Some of the last guy's blood had gotten into her mouth. The thought made her want to retch.

"Drop the weapons." The guard on her left ordered.

One of them had their rifle trained on her while the other had theirs aimed just past her shoulder at someone behind her.

Treegar tightened her grip on the knife and bent her knees, preparing to spring.

More guards filled the area behind the door. Her heart sank as her odds plummeted.

She heard a gun hit the floor behind her. She flinched as someone touched her shoulder.

Air hissed through her clenched teeth. She shook with the effort it took to loosen her grip on her precious little knife and allow it to clatter to the floor.

The guards didn't lower their weapons but the ones at the door nodded to someone out of view.

Wade walked into the doorway, guards flowing out of his path. He looked around the room, shoulders relaxed and posture reflecting an easy confidence. "Tsk, tsk, tsk. Now, what have you gone and done?" His question while stated lightly had a hard edge.

Treegar watched him warily, her focus tunnelling on to him despite the guns aimed at her. She shuffled back a half step.

"Looks like you've been busy." He looked behind her at the bed and then refocused on Treegar. His eyes were hard and he pushed his jaw forward. He half turned from her and then snapped back, his arm swinging in an arc ending at her face.

Treegar felt the sting on her cheek, her head's instinctive reaction to snap to the left with the force of the blow but she resisted it, stiffening her neck and staring at the hateful petty man before her.

"These were friends. You just moved yourself to the front of the line, missy." He turned to the guards, "take her, we're doing this now." The two guards inside the room jumped to lower their weapons and grab her.

Treegar twisted away from them and pushed her palm into the nose of the first one, breaking it but not successfully forcing the cartilage into his brain. He stumbled back but his companion managed to wrap his beefy hands around her left arm and pull her off balance. She kicked and bit at him, resorting to savage, primal actions in her attempt to extricate herself from his grip.

Someone hit the guard who held her, his grip loosened. She wrenched herself free, stumbling away and into Garner's arms. The pair stood in front of the scientists, shielding the corner they cowered in from the men at the door.

She took a moment to reassess the situation. The two guards that had reached for her were resuming their course, coming at her again but with greater caution. One had blood and snot gushing down his face, evidence of a very broken nose.

A gun went off. The sound made Treegar's hearing go fuzzy and her heart broke into a gallop.

"Settle down or the next one goes into one of your friends."

Treegar froze.

"That's better. Tie her up." Wade ordered, lowering the rifle that he had just shot.

The two guards grabbed her, ripping her from Garner's grasp, their hands squeezing her arms as hard as they could. Treegar could feel her hands begin to tingle from the restriction. Torn cloth was wrapped securely around her wrists, the material biting into her skin. The guards pushed her into the waiting hands of their companions at the door, who caught her and dragged her into the hall.

She stumbled and fell to her knees. Her struggles to stand were halted when a foot landed on her back knocking the air from her lungs and sending her to the floor. Someone stepped in front of her. Treegar craned her neck back to look up.

Wade glared down at her, his age and weight doing him no favours from this steep angle.

"I'm going to enjoy watching you burn."

Treegar felt around her mouth to gather sufficient saliva then spat it at him. The bloody glob arched and missed his face entirely, landing with a splat between his boots. She glared, wishing for her little knife so she could attack him, kill the root of their problem rather than the symptoms.

Wade sneered, "Pick her up, let's get going."

The guards grabbed her under her arms and hauled her to her feet. Treegar resisted as best she could, dropping her body to the floor so the men had to lift her full weight. She refused to plant her feet under her, making them drag her down the corridor behind Wade. She wished she had her boots back on now, her sock shod feet doing almost nothing to inhibit her captors progress.

Wade strode through the front door, leaving the door open behind him.

Treegar hooked her feet on the inside of the frame, pulling her body back from her captors. The guards yanked on her armpits, pitting their weight against the strength of her feet. She could feel her feet slipping so she released her hold. This sent the guards stumbling forward with her, crashing into Wades back and sending them all into the snow.

Treegar rolled with the fall, pulling free of the guards. The wet snow soaked her clothing and feet in an instant but her body left a pink smear of blood behind her. She sprang to her feet while her guards and Wade were still reacting to the fall. She kicked Wade in the face, her foot connecting with the side of his head in a dull thud.

She then lashed out at the guards, hitting one with a glancing kick. She pivoted and sent a swift kick to the second guard's jaw, her foot slipping on the sloppy ground and making her over balance. Unable to use her arms to balance she tumbled forward and slammed Wade.

There was scrambling all around her. A guard grabbed her from behind and hauled her up, wrestling her into a tight hold while the original guards and Wade righted themselves. They were all soaked and covered in mud and blood.

"Bring the rabbit!" Wade roared. He was cradling one side of his face and glaring at her with intense hatred. His skin was nearly purple and he shook either from emotion or the cold. A guard was deferentially helping him walk over to her.

"You're going to melt from the inside out." He hissed into her ear, his hot breath licking the side of her face.

A guard returned with a plastic bowl. Wade reached out with his gloved right hand and plucked a chunk of raw meat from the top.

"Did you know that you can be infected from the meat? Doesn't matter if the creature is still moving or not, one touch," He smirked, though the swelling on his right side made motion less menacing than he may have intended, "and you're gone. Now, how about you take a bite, you must be hungry after all that fighting, huh?"

Treegar's stomach rebelled. Beads of sweat dripped down the side of her face. Wade reached out with his left hand and dug his fingers into her jaw, trying to force it open. She clenched and shook her head. The person holding her tightened their hold and someone grabbed her hair to force her head still.

Wade's eyes glinted with enjoyment. He held the infected meat an inch from her face, waiting for her jaw to pop open so he could force it down her throat.

Treegar felt hyper aware of every millimeter between her and the meat. All it would take would be one brush of her skin, one mistake and she would be gone.

Wade's fingers dug deeper forcing the hinge of her jaw to pop open.

She gasped and ripped her head from the person holding her hair. She felt the searing pain of whole chunks of her hair being ripped out while she threw herself backward into her captor and away from Wade. She kicked out, her feet connecting with Wade and forcing him to stumble backward.

The person holding her slipped and sent them both rolling into the mud again. She rolled away as fast as she could and back on to her feet, wasting barely a second to look around her.

Her gaze fell first on her companions. Garner looked at her with a smile of admiration which sent shivers of delight running through her. Dr. Nagi looked at her with shocked wonder. Dr. Scordato wasn't looking at her. His gaze was locked in horror at where she had been.

Treegar followed his gaze.

Wade was on the ground. Both her captors were on the ground, one still clutching a chunk of hair and skin. The man holding the bowl of meat bits was on the ground.

It took Treegar's mind a split second to make the decision. Before her legs even moved, she was yelling, "Run!"

The guards holding her companions were slower to react than they were. Garner shouldered the one holding him and turned back to the house. Dr. Nagi lurched forward and out of her guard's distracted hold. Jason turned in his guard's hold and began running despite him. His guard dragged behind him for a moment and then released him and began running beside him.

Despite starting before them Treegar was the last to reach the door, her wet socks slipping on the sloppy ground. Garner held it open for her before pulling it closed and bolting it behind them.

Treegar looked through the window beside the door to see Wade begin to rise, a burn disfiguring the left side of his face.

26

It was the sum of its parts and separate from them. It lived within them and yet existed without them. While it hated the loss of one it could survive within one. And in the upheaval, survival was all that mattered.

*   *   *

The screams and moans of the infected echoed through the house punctuated by periodic gun shots.

"Pull those chairs over here. We need to barricade this door. And any other entrances!" Garner ordered.

Jason grabbed the nearest chair and rushed it to the door. He was followed by three other chairs all of which piled against the door.

"That won't hold for long, we need something heavier, sturdier." Jason observed. He tapped his finger against his thigh, "The dresser!" He exclaimed before turning and rushing to the bedroom.

Garner followed close behind and helped lift the solid piece. It was made of real wood and actually weighed more than Jason had expected it to. Together they maneuvered it over bodies and out to the door. Treegar and Jaspreet slid the chairs away and Jason gratefully dropped the heavy piece snuggly against the door.

Garner slid the chairs back in front of the dresser covered door, wedging one of them tightly against it.

"Wait!" Jason noticed that one of their guards had made it inside with them. "We can't just leave them out there!" Gunshots punctuated his words.

Treegar leveled him with a hard stare, "Are you volunteering to join them?"

The guard shook his head and backed down immediately.

"Where are the other entrances?" Garner demanded.

"In the back, through the kitchen."

"Any others?"

The man shook his head, "No, not that I know of."

Jason rushed down the hall, past the bedroom and the dead guards, into a room he only vaguely remembered from when they were bustled through and shoved into the pantry. A sliding glass door dominated one wall. The perfect entry point for infected. Jason cursed and grabbed the table, leveraging it to begin tilting it on its side.

Garner swore behind him and Jason suddenly felt the table lift more easily with the other man's help. With the table in place, they both stepped back and looked at the surrounding glass panels.

"Let's hope they are too busy for a little while to come at us." Garner pulled in his lower lip and began chewing on it. "We gotta get out of here, this place is a death trap."

"We need our gear." Jason said anxiously.

"Jaspreet and Treegar are looking. We need to plan an escape route."

Garner turned and moved back down the hallway, past the cringing guard and into the sitting room. Jason gave the barely blocked glass door a final fear-filled look before following.

Their bags were open and the contents piled about the room. The bits of meteorite lay on the coffee table like pieces to a jigsaw puzzle while blankets, the tent, the knives, and their other non-food supplies were sorted into piles. None of their food was in the room.

Treegar had her helmet locked back in place, her hands now free, and was stuffing supplies into her pack while Jaspreet pulled down her own visor. Jason hastily grabbed his own helmet and shoved it on, the tight confines lessening the rising panic. He then instinctively swept the pieces of meteorite off the table and into the bottom of his bag. He didn't have proof that they were the reason the infected behaved so strangely around their group, but he also wasn't going to rule that hypothesis out.

"How do you get out of the compound?" Garner asked the fidgeting guard.

"What? Oh, um... the front gate. But you can't open it."

"Why not?" Treegar demanded, looking as terrifying as ever with the closed visor intensifying the cold impassivity of her stare and drying blood smeared across her face.

The man froze for a moment, a distinctly deer in headlights look coming over his face before he stammered a reply, "B...because, someone has to be inside the g... gate t... to keep it open. It, ah, swings closed if you don't hold it there."

Jason raised his brow, "What if we jam its mechanism?"

The guard shook his head and then looked thoughtful.

"It's worth a shot. We need to check the kitchen and take what food we can carry. Gather all the guns you can find. We'll need them on our way out." Garner ordered.

"Guns?"

"Yeah, did you expect us to ask the infected to nicely move aside so we can leave?"

The guard looked back and forth between Garner and the others, but none of them contradicted him.

A gunshot rang out, sounding like it was right outside of the house. It made all of them jump and the guard looked around frantically, instinctively shuffling away from the sound. Treegar and Garner jumped into action, surging through the house with all thoughts of discussion ended. They ransacked cupboards and filled their bags to bursting before trading with Jaspreet and Jason and filling theirs as well.

When the bags were full the group turned their attention back to the guard, "Do you have protective clothing you can wear?" Jason asked, trying to phrase what he thought as an obvious question as gently as possible.

"Oh, um, yeah." He mumbled then turned and hurried back down the hall to the entryway and opened a closet. The door could only open halfway due to a chair blocking it but the man reached in anyway and began pulling out a winter coat.

Something hit the door causing the dresser and chairs to shake. It hit again. And again.

The man froze mid action then became frantic, pulling on his coat and hat. Within moments he was sprinting back to the kitchen.

The door took another hit. Jason took a last look at the door and verified that the dresser was holding, for now, and then moved to the bedroom. He quickly divested the dead men of their weapons, tucking Treegar's useful little knife into his pocket. Between the bodies he gathered three guns and three partial boxes of bullets.

There was a thud from the foyer. Jason whipped out of the bedroom to see that one of the chairs had fallen over. Then the door was hit again.

Jason turned and sprinted the few steps to the kitchen, clutching the guns and ammo to his chest. "We need to get going. They are hitting the front door hard."

Garner nodded but focused more on the guns and ammunition Jason was carrying. Jason dropped them on the counter and Garner and Treegar immediately began picking them over.

"Oh, this is for you." Jason held the little knife out to Treegar.

She looked at it and then looked at him. Her frown furrowed but her eyes were unusually soft. "Thanks." She reached out and took it, then bent down and slid it back into place in her boot.

Jason quirked a little smile. That was the closest he'd gotten to a friendly interaction with her in a while. Maybe she was human after all, even if it was the psychotic kind of human.

"Are there any more guns?" Garner asked.

Jason shook his head and then turned the question to the other man. "In the front room. Wade always kept a couple hidden there, just in case." He revealed before flushing and rushing down the hallway. Jason watched the man jump as the door was hit again and even in the kitchen, he could hear the sound of breaking wood.

The man returned with another two guns which were shared with the group. Garner ordered another quick search which took about five minutes and only turned up a full set of kitchen knives, which were equally shared out. The front door continued to be hammered, with increasing splintering.

Jason was just glad that the infected were focusing on the front door and hadn't explored around the house to find the kitchen door yet.

"Alright, let's make our way to the gate. If there are survivors, we help where we can, but our priority is getting out.

"Wouldn't it be better to clear out the infected? Won't opening the gate let others in?" The guards asked, his voice noticeably quivering as he spoke.

"You're welcome to stay." Treegar deadpanned.

"Look, we don't live here, we don't want to live here, and frankly, you were planning on killing us a few minutes ago. I am not sticking around to see if you will still want to do that after the immediate threat is gone. You can come with us or stay here, honestly, I don't care." Garner's tone was kind but firm and the man responded to it on an subconscious level. His shoulders drooped a little and he gave a slight nod with his chin.

"Let's go." Garner ordered.

The group formed their usual positions with the scientists in the middle and the soldiers ahead and behind. The guard settled in with Jason and Jaspreet but shied away from Treegar which put him in the middle.

They slid the table away from the door and Garner eased the handle down, slid the door open and stepped through. The back yard had no fencing which allowed them to move quickly and quietly away from the house. They moved along the fences of other houses, darting through open spaces and seeking cover.

Between the houses they could see the main road of the settlement. So far it looked deserted. Jason assumed that meant the infected were occupied attacking the homes people had fled into. Either that or they were stalking the sources of the periodic gun shots.

Jason kept his gun at the ready, copying his military companions. Unlike them, his heart was racing and he was trying to not think about the very real possibility that they might not make it out of here alive.

The row of houses ended at a tall wooden wall. Part of it consisted of living trees, while others were boards and panels nailed and screwed into place. "Which way?" Garner whispered to their former guard.

"Uh, turn right. If we follow the wall, it won't take long."

They turned right and did as he directed. As they went it became increasingly clear that the wall was built out of desperation, not coordination. Chunks of house siding had been used, along with doors and plastic sheeting. Holes were patched up with cutting boards and plastic planters.

They paused at the corner of a house; the gate stood about twenty feet away but between them it was a wide empty expanse. Garner eased his head around the corner snapping it back in an instant. "Four Infected. They didn't see me but killing them will draw more. How do we open the gate?" He pegged their new companion with a stare.

"It… it's just over th… there. Y… you just turn the leaver and the doors open. But you gotta hold it open, they swing shut once you let go.

Garner nodded at Treegar, "Don't worry about that, we'll take care of it. You just shoot straight. Don't waste your bullets."

Jaspreet raised her hand, "Excuse me. I think I should get to the gate."

Garner shook his head but Jaspreet continued.

"You're all better shots than me. I've never even fired a gun before. I'll be more use getting the gate open. I'll figure out a way to keep it open long enough for me to follow you.

Garner actually seemed to be considering her points.

Jason shook his head hoping that Garner would veto the plan.

Garner nodded and Jason's heart sank. How could he approve this madness? And yet, Jason didn't speak up. He just watched Jaspreet acknowledge the acceptance of her crazy plan and grit her teeth in preparation.

"On the count of three we step out and open fire. Jaspreet will sprint to the opening mechanism; You should go with her," He spoke to their former guard, "Keep the infected away while she works. Once it's open, both of you get out as fast as you can.

The man went pale under his face shield but nodded.

"One, two, three." Garner sprung from his position and landed in the street, gun raised and firing.

Jason followed after him with the others moving in behind. Around the corner he looked for an infected to shoot and found the little girl from earlier. His heart skipped in his chest and he hesitated for a single breathless moment. In that moment her head snapped to look at him and she began to sprint toward their group.

Jason fired. His first shot went wide but his second took her in the chest. She faltered as the bullet impacted but then continued. He got her in the head with his third shot and she dropped sliding till her corpse stopped only a few paces from him.

More infected replaced her, following the sound of gunfire to race toward their prey. Jason sighted another and pulled the trigger. He followed Garner as he sidestepped toward the gate, waiting anxiously for Jaspreet to perform a miracle.

Jason's gun clicked in his hand, useless. He looked over at Jaspreet and sprinted to her side just as the gate began to open.

"Give me your gun." He held out his hand and eyed the mechanism. It consisted of rope attached through a series of pulleys to the gate. When a wheel was turned the rope pulled the gate till it bent away from its natural curve and forced itself open. Holding the wheel kept it open but the moment it was released the structure would snap back into place.

"I'm a little busy." Jaspreet ground out through her clenched teeth.

"I can see that. Let me take over." He reached out and took the wheel from her, turning it more easily than she had.

"It's open, jam it and let's get out of here." Their former guard snapped at them.

Jaspreet looked at Jason. "Give it to me and go."

"What? No! Give me something to jam it with."

She shook her head. "I don't have anything. Go. You need to get those rings to Agatha's girls, remember?"

He shook his head, "Not at the cost of your life!"

She gave him a sad smile. "I knew what I volunteered for."

"Oh for crying out loud." Their guard cried and shouldered between them, shoving Jason from the wheel and catching it himself. "Get out of here, both of you. I'm staying. This is my home. Get out."

Jason shook his head, "You can't!"

"Shut up and get going! I want to close this gate and get rid of these things. You want to take your chances out there? Fine, I'm taking my chances here."

Jason hesitated.

"Go!"

Jaspreet leaned toward him, "Thank you, and I'm sorry." She turned and sprinted through the opening.

Jason gave the man one last look before following her. He slipped through the opening just before it slammed shut. The gust of air emphasizing his passage.

"Where's our friend?" Garner asked.

"He chose to stay behind," Jaspreet answered softly.

There were more gunshots behind them.

"He wanted to take his chances there." Jason repeated.

Garner and Treegar nodded, "Then we'd better get going. All this noise will attract things."

*   *   *

The world sank into gloomy twilight while Treegar and the group hiked south-west from Salvation until they reached the top of a ridge. They hadn't heard a gunshot for at least the past hour and the light was fading fast. Treegar could feel the adrenaline slipping away, only to be replaced by a deep fatigue.

She stumbled through the motions of setting their tent up, aided where possible by her equally exhausted companions. With their shelter stable, she crawled inside.

They had survived, somehow, and against all odds. She sent a silent prayer of thanks to Garner's God and an apology for all the blood on her hands.

27

It began to ease control. Allowing the bodies to move on their own, only forcing them to continue. This allowed it a separation from their individual and collective pain and hunger. It could see further, focus more clearly this way and its bodies continued as it desired.

*   *   *

Charissa wedged a piece of wood under the door knob to force it closed. It wasn't the most elegant solution but it was better than leaving the door open for the infected. Ryosuke's friend had been right, the infected would be drawn here after all that gunfire. She slid down with her back pressed to the door and stared down at the stairs to the basement.

Murderer.

Charissa flinched at the word. Shoving the thought away.

Killer.

Monster.

The words kept coming, accusing and denouncing her. The labels burned in her throat and bile rose. Her stomach revolted against the rest of her being.

Five people were dead because of her.

Penelope had returned to the kids immediately, leaving Charissa alone to deal with the door, the bodies of the intruders, and whatever was coming next.

It flooded her. Overwhelming her senses. Her breathing came in short and fast, black spots forming at the edge of her vision. Murderer.

The blood on her hands and arms pulled at her skin as it dried, creating a dirty crawling feeling. The smell of gunpowder clung to her clothing and clogged her nose. The chill air seeped through her layers caressing her like death. Monster.

This wasn't like neutralizing the infected. That was terrible but at least she could justify it to herself. She was serving the greater good. She was making the world safer for Sophia and Atticus. But this…

They attacked us. They threatened Sophia. They were stealing our food. They shot Timothy.

And yet.

She felt empty, dirty.

She knew she had no other choice. Or did she?

And now there were five corpses in their home. How were they ever to get them out?

Timothy… could he even survive?

Charissa moved to sit on the stairs in front of the door and felt a tidal wave of emotion rise up and engulf her. Tears swarmed over her vision and ran hot tracks down her cheeks. She shoved off her welding visor and threw it to the side, quickly followed by her bloodied gloves. With those items discarded she was able to freely rub at her eyes, swiping at the stream of tears with impatience.

"Aunty?" Sophia's high pitched voice broke through the silence.

Charissa turned and looked up the stairs.

"Daddy's asking for you." She said simply and then turned and ran back down the hall.

Charissa grit her teeth and turned, bracing her hands against one of the higher steps and pushing herself to her feet. The few short steps to the main floor had never felt so long though she raced to ascend them.

She passed the body of the first man she killed, keeping her eyes averted but picking her way around his growing pool of blood. The bedroom door was open. She could hear Atticus crying noisily. Charissa paused in the doorway and took in the scene.

Penelope was cradling Addicus while still holding Timothy's hand. Timothy was pale. Looking like a ghost already. Sophia sat on the other side of her father, pressing down on his stomach with all her might, as though she alone stood between him and death. She wasn't crying but her eyes were sunken and scared.

Timothy twitched and clenched his jaw to contain a gasp. His eyes strayed from his family and landed on Charissa. With a weary nod he motioned for her to come join them.

"Chary…" He whispered, although it came out airier and more strained than his normal voice. "You're here." His breath was shallow and laboured.

Charissa knelt beside Sophia, placing her hands over those of the little girl. Timothy gasped but gave her a small nod. "How you doing, Champ?" She murmured, keeping her words light even though her throat was thick with tears and emotion.

He gave her a small smile. "Never better." It was a baldfaced lie and they all knew it. Atticus' cries increased in pitch and even Sophie began to let tears slide down her face.

Beads of sweat were forming on his forehead and his eyes seemed unable to fully focus. He opened and closed his mouth several times.

He grew paler by the second and Charissa began to wonder if the pressure on his wound was doing anything at all. He turned his head from Charissa to Penelope. His eyes grew more intense and

Charissa looked away from his face to that of her sister.

Penelope looked simultaneously broken and fierce. She looked like she would fight death with her bare hands if only she could.

"Love… you." Timothy croaked.

Penelope's jaw clenched and her eyes shone with a fierce fire, "I love you too." She stated, as though it was a fact of the universe, so simple and true it didn't need repeating.

"Love you, Atti."

Atticus pulled his face out of his mothers neck where it had been buried and looked at his dad. Charissa's heart squeezed at the abject heartbreak in the little boy's face. "I love you too daddy!" he exclaimed.

Timothy nodded and forced a small smile before turning to his daughter. "I love you Soph." He seemed to rally a bit of strength, his words clearer this third time.

"I love you too Daddy!" Sophia wailed, pulling her hands from under Charissa's and throwing them around her Fathers neck.

He smiled a weary but genuine smile and finally locked eyes with Charissa again. "Protect them."

She nodded, accepting the transfer of responsibility.

He nodded and let his eyes drift closed. Charissa could feel his breathing slow beneath her hands and then, in the space between one heartbeat and the next, he was gone. His whole body seemed to sink into itself.

Penelope gasped and Sophia squeezed harder at his neck, pulling his now limp head tighter to her.

"No!" Penelope's voice broke on the word. She pulled Atticus tight to her chest and stared at the now lifeless body of her husband, the fire within her extinguished as suddenly as his had been.

To be continued.

9 781068 999307